MÁ
9

17/11/12.

JUNIOR

Please return/renew this item by the last date shown

worcestershire
countycouncil
Libraries & Learning

10 BEST HORROR STORIES EVER!

Michael Cox

SCHOLASTIC

Scholastic Children's Books,
Euston House, 24 Eversholt Street,
London NW1 1DB, UK

A division of Scholastic Ltd
London ~ New York ~ Toronto ~ Sydney ~ Auckland
Mexico City ~ New Delhi ~ Hong Kong

First published in the UK by Scholastic Ltd, 2000
(as *Top Ten: Horror Stories*)
This edition published 2009

ISBN 978 1407 11034 9

Page layout services provided by Quadrum Solutions Ltd, Mumbai, India
Printed and bound in the UK by CPI Bookmarque, Croydon, Surrey

2 4 6 8 10 9 7 5 3 1

Papers used by Scholastic Children's Books are made from
woods grown in sustainable forests.

CONTENTS

INTRODUCTION

Zombies! Vampires! Werewolves! Mad scientists! Fifty-foot killer tomatoes! They get *everywhere*, don't they. Well, they do if you're a *fear* fan. But just a moment. Before we go any further we better get something sorted. Maybe you don't *like* horror stories? Perhaps they leave you trembling from head to toe, drenched in cold sweat, with your hair standing on end, too frightened even to go to the bathroom that you're absolutely *desperate* to visit. In which case ... listen ... and *be warned*! If you're the sort who a) is terrified of kittens; b) sleeps with the light on; c) gets up every 15 minutes during the night to check that a horrendous, scaly, bloodsucking 'thing' hasn't crawled under your bed and is about to creep under the duvet with you; and d) has to get to the bottom of the stairs before the upstairs loo has finished flushing (ha! thought we didn't know about *that*, didn't you!) ... you better read no further. You'll find the cuddly pony stories on the next shelf.

OK! That's got rid of the wimps. Now we can get on with the *really* horrible stuff...

People have been enjoying horror stories ever since the first cave woman told her trembling kids about the huge, slobbering, knuckleheaded monster that was lurking in a dark and smelly corner of their cave just metres from where they were sitting – which wasn't a very nice way to talk about their father, was it? And ever since then, people have been scaring each other witless with all sorts of terrifying tales of odious ogres, maniacal monsters and bloodthirsty beasts.

During the last couple of centuries, horror story writing has *really* taken off. Hundreds of terror-ifically talented, imaginative, overexcitable horror writers have been burning the midnight oil to produce terrifying tales and scary stories that will frighten the teeth out of anyone who is brave enough to read them. When you really start to explore the terror-trove of books on the shelves you'll find them groaning (and occasionally screaming!) with all sorts of terrifying treats. Enormous homemade monsters, strange people who change in an instant from a faithful friend to a frenzied fiend (and no, we *haven't* met your teacher), killer crabs the size of supermarkets, screwy scientists who just can't wait to get their greasy mitts on your favourite and most delicate internal organs, tentacle-waving aliens who'll suck out your eyeballs at the drop of a spaceship!

So, for your utmost terror and deepest dread, here are ten of the best, hand-picked horror stories. Some are mega-famous and some not quite so famous, but they've all been retold in new (and absolutely disgusting) ways ... with a few laughs to tickle your chuckle buds. And just to make sure you're fully prepared for the horrors you're about to encounter there are some fearsome fact sections too. If you're not sure how to waste a werewolf, zap a zombie, or vanquish a vampire, don't worry! There are oodles of absolutely essential information about beating bad-guy bogeymen along with stacks of facts about horror writers, horror movies and fear itself.

OK! Hurry home with this book, get out your torch, your bunch of garlic and your sharpened stake ... switch out the lights, and prepare to give yourself a *write* fright.

Oh, and by the way. You know that assistant in the corner of the bookshop – yes *that's* the one – the one who's been watching you all the time you've been reading this introduction. Well, have you noticed the way they keep licking their lips, and the way their eyes look a bit pink and bloodshot, and the way their breath's coming in short excitable bursts? Perhaps it might be a good idea to avoid *their* till. You can never be too careful, can you!

STORY 1: THE HOUND OF THE BASKERVILLES

The first scary story that bounds, snapping and snarling into our totally terrifying Ten Best Ever is *The Hound of the Baskervilles* (1902) by Sir Arthur Conan Doyle (1859–1930). It's a horror story *and* a detective story. The Baskerville family are said to be haunted by a hideous, gigantic dog which roams Dartmoor in Devon. When Sir Charles Baskerville is found dead it's feared the horrendous hound has struck again. But why? And how? There's only one man who could possibly get to the bottom of the mystery and that's top detective Sherlock Holmes, as always aided by his trusty sidekick, Dr Watson. If that horrible hound had been around today this terrible case would certainly have featured on the TV crime-busting programme known as...

Sir Arthur Conan Doyle

Nick Villains: Evening all. We begin tonight's programme with a very, very scary case. Here in the studio, to tell us about it, we have ace detective and pipe smoker, Sherlock Holmes. Sherlock, it's a really horrible one, isn't it?

Sherlock Holmes: Yes, Nick. It is. It concerns Sir Charles Baskerville who was recently found dead outside his big posh mansion on his Dartmoor estate. The other day I was visited by Dr Mortimer, the Baskervilles' family doctor who examined the body. He seems to think that Sir Charles was *frightened* to death by something very, very, very *horrible*. To back up this theory, he gave me this ancient manuscript to study. I'll read it to you:

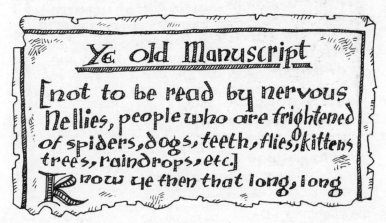

Ye old Manuscript

[not to be read by nervous Nellies, people who are frightened of spiders, dogs, teeth, flies, kittens, trees, raindrops, etc.] Know ye then that long, long ago, wicked Sir Hugo Baskerville and his [not quite so] wicked mates did kidnap a pretty local wench what he fancied somethin' rotten! While they were getting sozzled, the wench did run off home across the moor. Sir Hugo set off after 'er with his pack of hounds, saying he would give his soul to the powers of evil if they would 'elp him catch 'er. His mates followed some minutes later. After a mile or so they came across a fearcrazed shepherd who said he had seen the girl with the pack chasin' after 'er followed by Sir Hugo with a gigantic, 'orrible, dog "thing" snappin' at his heels! Not long afterwards they found the body of the poor maid, all dead of terror and tiredness! Close by lay Sir Hugo, a twitchin' and a jerkin' and a screamin' on account of the fact that a great black creature, at least the size of a small horse, with dribblin' jaws and blazin' eyes, was busy rippin' out 'is throat! The lads rode off, shrieking with terror. Later, one of them died of fright and the rest went completely doolally because of the 'orrid thing they 'ad seen. Since that day a monstrous hell-hound is said to have plagued the Baskervilles.

The End

Betty Dunnit: Oooer! That's *some* story! So, Sherlock, do you think there's a link between the old chap's death and this legendary 'devil-dog' that's said to terrorize the Baskerville family?

Sherlock: You bet, Betty. Dr Mortimer told me he visited Sir Charles a few weeks before his death. As they were chatting on the doorstep of Baskerville Hall he noticed the old chap go all pale and wobbly as he seemed to 'spot something' in the distance. Dr Mortimer turned round just in time to see what looked like 'a large black calf' passing across the drive. And that's not all. After Sir Charles's death, Dr Mortimer found a set of tracks next to his body. They were enormous and could only have been made by a *gigantic hound*.

Nick: So what's your next move, Sherlock?

Sherlock: Well Nick, Sir Charles Baskerville's heir and nephew, Sir Henry, has come to London from Canada. In a few days' time he's travelling down to Dartmoor to take over the Baskerville Estate. I'm sending my trusty friend, Dr Watson, to be his minder. I'm too busy to go but I know that Watson will guard him with his life.

Nick: Good old Watson!

Sherlock: Can I just add, Nick, that since Sir Henry's been here, two odd things have happened. First, he's had one of his brown boots stolen from his hotel room; and second, he's received a mysterious note warning him not to go to Dartmoor.

13

Betty: Hmm, *most* intriguing. Keep us informed, Sherlock. And viewers, if you know anything about the missing brown boot, that note, or the monstrous legendary devil-dog ... let us know! You can ring us on our hotline – here's the number:

K9K9K9!

Some weeks later...

WUFF JUSTICE UPDATE

Nick Villains: Evening all. Tonight we bring you the latest on the Baskerville case. We've not been able to speak to busy Sherlock Holmes but we have got copies of the letters that have passed between Watson and him. So here's the story so far:

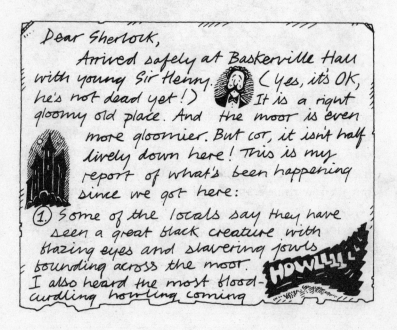

> Dear Sherlock,
>   Arrived safely at Baskerville Hall with young Sir Henry. (Yes, it's OK, he's not dead yet!) It is a right gloomy old place. And the moor is even more gloomier. But cor, it isn't half lively down here! This is my report of what's been happening since we got here:
> (1) Some of the locals say they have seen a great black creature with blazing eyes and slavering jowls bounding across the moor. HOWLLLL
> I also heard the most blood-curdling howling coming

from up there at night. Do you think that it could be ... it?!

(2.) A really dangerous convict called Selden has escaped from Dartmoor Prison. He is hiding out on the moor and everyone is terrified that he will get them.

(3.) Last night I heard a woman crying somewhere in the house.

(4.) Yesterday I went to the GLUGGG part of the moor known as Grimpen Mire. I saw a pony slip into the mud. Next moment it was gone. Just like that. Slurp, slurp... glug!

There is something very odd indeed going on here, Sherlock, but I can't make head nor toe-nail of it?! Wish you were here! Toodle pip old thing!

Love
Watson

P.S. I have met an insect collector called Stapleton. He is a very decent sort. He lives in a cottage near Grimpen Mire.

P.P.S. Have just checked Sir Henry again. STILL alive! Doing well aren't I?

Dear Watson

Well done! Do not worry about not being able to understand what's going on. We can't all be as clever as what I am. Just keep looking after Sir Henry. So go and check on him ... now!

All the best. Sherlock

Sherlock!

You wouldn't believe the stuff that's been going on down here! The other night me and Sir Henry heard a kerfuffle in the corridor. We went to investigate and found the maidservant waving a candle about at the window. There was another light waving back at her from the hillside opposite. Sherlock! She is the escaped convict's sister. It was her I heard sobbing. She has been leaving food and clothing near the old hut up there.

After he'd given her a ticking off, Sir Henry turned to me and said, "By thunder, Watson, we will go and catch him!" We hadn't been out long when we heard that awful howling, growling, moaning sound and my blood ran cold. I asked Sir Henry if he wanted to turn back and he said 'No. by thunder!' (He's very fond of saying this.) In the end we missed the convict but we did see a tall thin figure all lit up in the moonlight standing on the rock above the hut. I wonder who THAT could be? It certainly wasn't the convict because he is a short chubby chap.

                    Watson.

P.S. Just to let you know, I've just checked Sir Henry. He is still alive.

P.P.S. Wish you were here. This all gets more puzzling and scary by the moment.

Nick: It certainly does! So much so that *we've* decided to be there. We're sending our very own Betty Dunnitt down to Dartmoor to see if she can get to the bottom of this mystery. Frightened of dogs are you, Betty?

A few days later…

WUFF JUSTICE (LIVE)

Betty Dunnit: You join mc here on gloomy Dartmoor at a most interesting moment. I am crouched behind a rock with Dr Watson … watching 'the old hut'!

 Dr Watson: I have seen a boy taking food to this hut a few times. So I reckon that the convict must be hiding in there. I am going in to arrest him!

17

Betty Dunnit: After you, Dr Watson. You brave thing!
Dr Watson: Come on out, you convict chappy. Or I'll give you a taste of this pistol!
A voice: Don't shoot, Watson!
Watson: Well bless my soul! *Holmes!* What are you doing in there?
Holmes: Watson, what a chump you are! I've been here all the time! Ever since you came down with Sir Henry.
Watson: By jingo! So *you* were the tall, skinny bloke we saw in the moonlight.
Holmes: Less of the skinny, Watson! Yes, it *was* me. I've been hiding out in the old hut and doing some snooping. And guess what I've found out. I now know that the...

Betty Dunnit: By thunder! What's that?
Holmes: If I'm not mistaken it's the ... **hell-hound!**

And it sounds like it's got someone. Watson! Where did you put Sir Henry?

Watson: Oooh cripes! Now let me see? I *think* I left him at, er...?

Holmes: Watson, you great big nitwit! What *have* you gone and done, you *drip*! Quick, everyone! Follow me!

Watson: Pant pant! Gasp gasp! Oh no! Look! That body laying face down over there. It's Sir Henry! I'd recognize that thatched tweed suit and those green wellies anywhere!

Holmes: Oh no! Sob sob! You've gone and blown it now, Watson. You've only gone and got our poshest client *ever*, eaten by a monster-dog! And live on *Wuff Justice*! Brilliant, Watson! Just brilliant! How will I ever live this down. I'm finished. Lend me your gun, will you? I think I'll just blow my brains out now...

Betty Dunnit: Looks like the poor bloke's almost had his face chewed off. The only thing it's not touched is this dirty great beard of his...

Holmes: BEARD! Did you say *beard*?! Sir Henry hasn't got a ... *beard*!!

Watson: Here, let's have a gander. I'll just roll him over a bit more and ... HA HA! YIPPPEE! OH GOODY GOODY! It's *not* Sir Henry! It's Selden, the escaped convict! I remember now, Sir Henry gave some of his old togs to the maid. She must have given them to her brother to wear so the hell-hound mistook him for a Baskerville! Ha ha ha! Hip hip hoorah!

Betty Dunnit: This is Betty Dunnit with two very happy chums and one very dead convict, returning you to the studio!

Nick: Serves him right. Nasty little convict! Well, viewers, that *was* exciting, wasn't it! So, what *has* Holmes discovered? Tune in to *Wuff Justice* to find out, soon!

Some more days later…

WUFF JUSTICE (EVEN LIVER)

Betty Dunnit: Good evening, everyone! We're going straight over to Baskerville Hall. Nick's there with Sherlock Holmes and Dr Watson. There've been some really *stunning* developments since I was last down there, haven't there, Nick?

Nick: Certainly have, Betty. But … *thank Sherlock!* … I think this one's just about all wrapped up now. He's going to update us on what's happened since that terrible business with the convict. Spill the beans, maestro!

Sherlock: Well, Nick, once we'd handed the convict's body over to the local cops, Watson and I came back here to Baskerville Hall and I told him how I'd discovered that Stapleton, the insect collector, was not who he said he was, but really a distant relative of the Baskervilles.

Nick: Hmmmm, *very* suspicious!

Watson: That's just what we thought.

Sherlock: And now Stapleton has invited Sir Henry to have drinks with him at his cottage this very evening.

Nick: Hmmm, even *more* suspicious!

Sherlock: So I've told Sir Henry that *he* must go but that *we* can't as we're going back to London on urgent business.

Watson: But we aren't really! Tee hee! Cunning, aren't we?

Sherlock: Instead we're going to sneak up to the cottage and see what happens.

Nick: Oooh! Can I come with you?

Sherlock: Yes, Nick. But it won't be a picnic, Nick. And we must be quick, Nick.

Betty: Oooer!... This is *exciting*, isn't it? While the chaps are making their way to the cottage there'll just be time for the item on the Luton toilet-seat thief, then we'll go straight back to Dartmoor.

Nick: Welcome back, everyone. You join us here outside Stapleton's cottage. We're crouched by the path and a mist is falling. So I don't think there's much chance of us being spotted. The cottage curtains are open so we can clearly see Stapleton and Sir Henry chatting by the fire.

Sherlock: Look chaps! Stapleton's just handed Sir Henry a brandy. And now he's leaving the room.

Watson: It looked more like a whisky to me!

Sherlock: Shut up, Watson! Now look! Stapleton's coming out of the house. He's going to the big shed in the orchard and ... unlocking the door?

Watson: And now he's going back into the cottage.

Nick: Hey! Sir Henry's putting on his coat. It looks like he's about to leave for home. Stapleton's come back into the room. They're shaking hands.

Sherlock: Just as I thought! The cunning blighter. Now chaps, keep very still! Sir Henry will be passing us at any moment...

Nick: Here he comes!

Sir Henry (to himself): Brrrrrr ... what a chilly evening ... *tum tee tum tee tum.*

Watson: There he goes...

Nick: What on earth's *that*!

Sherlock: It's coming, Watson! Get out your pistol! NOW!

Watson: By the cringe! Look at *that*!

Nick: Oooh mother! What an *enormous* dog! It must be at least as big as a ... *donkey*!

Sherlock: And it's after ... *Sir Henry*!!!

Sir Henry: *Aaagh! By Thunder! Aaaaaaagh! Gerrritoffff-ameeee!*

Sherlock: Now, Watson! Now! Let him have it!

Watson: Which one? The dog ... or Sir Henry?

Sherlock: The dog! You dipstick!

whimper whimper whimper wh...

Nick: Nice shooting, Sherlock! Hard luck, Watson.

Sherlock: What a brute! But by the way it's rolling on its back and waving its paws in the air I should say it's a goner. *...whimper whimper. Uuurgh!*

Nick: Look! Someone's climbing over the back fence of the cottage!

Watson: It's Stapleton! He's doing a runner! Should I go after him, Sherlock?

Sherlock: No, leave him, Watson. He's headed for the mire. In this mist he'll *never* find his way across.

Stapleton: Oh sugar!

Slurp slurp slurp … glug … glug … glug … glug…

Sherlock: Told you … didn't I.

Watson (quietly): Bloomin' know all.

A few more days later…

WUFF JUSTICE ROUNDUP

Betty: Good evening! You join us here at Baskerville Hall for our *final* look at the case of the Hound of the Baskervilles. And all's well that end's well! The monster dog's dead. Sir Henry's recovered from his ordeal…

Sir Henry: Certainly have, Betty!

Watson: And Stapleton's at the bottom of the bog!

Nick: Where he belongs! It jolly well served the bounder right!

Sherlock: It certainly did, Nick. For it was him who frightened old Sir Charles to death by setting that monstrous dog on him and making him believe it was the legendary Hound of the Baskervilles. His plan was to get rid of the last two living Baskervilles then claim the estate for himself.

Nick: So this huge creature wasn't the legendary hell-hound then?

Sherlock: Don't be thick, Nick! Of course it wasn't. It was just a very big, old-fashioned kind of dog that you can still get if you're prepared to shop around a bit. Stapleton had trained it to attack the Baskervilles by giving it bits of their clothing to sniff. That's why he stole that old brown boot of Sir Henry's from the hotel in London. There's no such thing as the Hound of the Baskervilles. It's nothing more than a load of superstitious old codswallop!

All: By thunder! What was *that*?!

THE END

FANTASTIC FACTS 1: THE CREATURE FEATURE

Horror stories are full of horrendous animals like the Hound of the Baskervilles. So prepare to go '*aaah*' (or maybe 'AAAAAAAARGH') as you meet ten more animal terrors (all straight out of the pet shop from hell!):

1 BALAOO – THE DEMON BABOON

Appearance An ape-like creature who wears a man's clothes.

Where found Paris, France in the early 1900s.

Behaviour Scary! Weird! Balaoo is a baboon who has been operated on by a mad scientist. By joining up a couple of nerve endings under Balaoo's tongue the barmy boffin has given him the power of speech. Yes, just like that! Balaoo terrorizes all of Paris by swinging through the trees and grabbing girls by their hair. He then drags them up into the trees and swings off with them. Apart from the one who happened to be wearing a wig.

Well deserved doom There are lots of Balaoo stories. In the one above he ends up on a roof-top bunging bricks at the crowd below until he is killed by a sharpshooter. But then we find out it's not him but another ape who just happens to be on the run from the zoo. The real Balaoo has done a runner! Moral – don't kill off your best character if you want your best-selling baboon to run and run.

Watch it! In *'Balaoo ou des pas au Plafond'* (1913) based on the newspaper series of Gaston Laroux.

2 THE WHITE WORM

Appearance On good days, a posh woman called Lady Arabella March. She has a sweet, hissing sort of voice and long, white, snaky fingers. She likes to dress in soft, white stuff. But that's when she's in *human form*!

She's much more at home when she's worm shaped, and turns into an enormous slippery, wet, serpenty thing whenever she feels like it!

Where found The bottom of a deep, wet and very pongy hole – it smells like a cross between a tank full of drowned rats and the clogged drains of an abandoned slaughterhouse. (Use your imagination.)

Behaviour Fond of wrapping her thin white wormy arms around victims and pulling them into the hole, then doing all sorts of disgusting things to them.

Well deserved doom Finally destroyed by plucky next door neighbour, Adam Salton. He fills the hole with dynamite which explodes when it's ignited by a spark of lightning. After which, loads of grot, gunge and slime comes bubbling up with Lady Arabella floating on top of it. That'll learn her!

Read all about it! In *The Lair of the White Worm* (1911) by Bram Stoker, the author of *Dracula*.

3 THE BIRDS

Appearance Perfectly normal dicky-birds: robins, finches, larks, gulls, etc.

Where found Britain (in the book); USA (in the film).

Behaviour Huge flocks of otherwise normal birds begin attacking human beings all over the place. They're almost unstoppable. In a terrifying scene in the film they attack a group of schoolchildren. (Nature walks will never be the same again!) People barricade themselves inside their houses but the relentless birds peck and tear their way in. (This door's solid oak ... send for the woodpeckers!)

Read all about it! In the short story, 'The Birds' (1952) by Daphne du Maurier.

Watch it! In the film *The Birds* (1963), by the great suspense- and horror-film director, Alfred Hitchcock. How did Alfred get all those thousands of birds to put in such brilliant performances? He must have had them eating out of his hand!

4 KING KONG

Appearance Giant gorilla.

Where found Skull Island, but he's captured by a movie company and taken to New York.

Behaviour Sloppy ... followed by *stroppy*! Falls in love with a blonde actress. (It'll never work, they can't agree on a colour scheme for the cage.) Goes to a photo shoot with her. Thinks she's being attacked when photographers' flashbulbs pop. Goes berserk and destroys huge chunk of New York.

Undeserved doom Zapped by dive bombers and machine-guns. Tragic and totally unnecessary. They should have just gently blown up his nose – with their breath, not with bombs!

Watch it! In the movie *King Kong* (1933), which was remade in 1976, and again in 2005 ... but the first one's the best!

5 THE CRAB MONSTERS

Appearance Giant crabs. (Bet you'd never have guessed!)

Where found An island in the Pacific Ocean where odd things are happening: earthquakes, tidal waves, disappearing scientists.

Behaviour Atrocious! You certainly wouldn't take them home to tea. The crabs have been affected by atomic radiation, and they've been eating the disappearing scientists. ('Oh no, mum! Not *scientist-paste* sandwiches again!') By absorbing the scientists they acquire their brain-power and voices. A new team of scientists arrives to investigate. They too are lured to their deaths by the crab monsters who call to them in the night, pretending to be their dead pals.

Well deserved doom Just when it looks like all the scientists are going to become crab meat, they discover that the crabs can be destroyed by electricity. Using shock tactics, they kill all but one crab – a giant pregnant female. In the end, Hank the heroic (but tragically thick) scientist brings a power cable down on top of the final crab monster and they both die fizzily.

Watch it! (If you dare!) In the film *Attack of the Crab Monsters* (1957).

6 THE RATS IN THE WALLS

Appearance Fat, furry and ratty. There are thousands of them – a huge 'army'!

Where found At Exham Priory in England. First of all they're only 'heard', scurrying and scraping and squeaking, inside the walls. All this gets a bit much for the new owner and his cat, so he organizes an expedition to find out what's going on. Along with some chums, including 'plump' Captain Norrys, they go beneath the priory. To their horror, they discover a massive, ancient, underground town, full of skeletons. It seems that long, long ago, pens full of people were kept down here and fattened up for some sort of ancient, cannibalistic, sacrifice ritual! (And you thought it was just going to be full of old gardening tools and paint cans.)

Behaviour At some point in the past, the rat army has attacked and eaten the people in the pens then rampaged out of the priory and attacked the local peasants. Just as the rats now attack the new owner, his cat and Captain Norrys, when they become separated from the other members of the expedition. Three hours later the owner awakes to find himself crouched over the half-eaten body of Captain Norrys. His own cat is clawing and tearing at his throat.

And did they meet their doom? Most probably not! Rats are born survivors, not to mention lucky. After this terrible tragedy, Exham Priory is blown up by the authorities. The very same ones who believe that it was *the new owner* who killed and ate Captain Norrys! As he now sits and wonders what has become of his cat, he can *still* hear the rats in the walls. Except *this* time, they're in the walls of his padded cell at the lunatic asylum!

Read all about it! In 'The Rats in the Walls' (1923) by H P Lovecraft.

7 CATERPILLARS

Appearance Each one fat and fleshy, at least 30 centimetres long. Greyish-green in colour and slightly luminous. Do not have sucker-type feet like normal caterpillars but rows of pincers, like crabs. No proper faces, just a mouth. Covered all over in odd lumps and swellings.

Where found In a house and garden in Italy.

Behaviour Like to go around in a huge, slithering, pyramid-shaped mass. A great carpet of the horrible things squeezes and creeps its way into the bedroom of a man who has deliberately trodden on and killed a smaller sort of caterpillar earlier in the day. Soon afterwards he contracts a horrible fatal illness.

Read all about it! In EF Benson's short story 'Caterpillars' (1912).

8 THE FLY

Appearance A man with the head of a fly and a fly's leg where his right arm should be. His head is white and hairy, his ears are pointed, his moist pink nose is like that of a huge cat, his eyes are two saucer-shaped brown bumps and his mouth is a vertical slit with a dripping, black trunk hanging out of it. (Yeah! ... eat your heart out, Leonardo di Caprio!)

Behaviour Disturbed, desperately unhappy. The fly-man is a scientist who has learned how to teleport things across space with a machine that breaks them down into their molecules, then puts them back together again when they've arrived. He decides to transmit himself but, as he does, a fly gets into the machine and he ends up with a few fly body-parts ('So what! *I'm* stuck with the guy's head!' – the fly.)

Undeserved doom He's so cheesed off with his appearance that he sticks his horrible head under a giant steam hammer and asks his wife to throw the switch. She does. Splatt! End of horrendous head.

End of scientist. End of wife. She commits suicide. Did it have to end like that? Why didn't he just grow a beard or something?

Read all about it! In the short story 'The Fly' (1957) by George Langham.

But *don't* watch it! (Unless you're old enough!) Film versions: 1958 and 1986.

9 THE THING

Appearance Three mad, blazing hate-filled eyes. A face surrounded by blue worms, crawling and writhing where hair should be. The shaft of an ice-axe sticking out of its split skull. All encased in a block of ice. (But not for long!)

Where found Near the North Pole, in a huge crater made by an alien craft.

Behaviour Very quiet, while it remains in its block of ice. But then the scientists who've found it decide to thaw it out. It escapes and wanders off with its brains oozing greenly out of the split in its skull (nice). It attacks the husky dogs and scientists. And whatever it attacks, it *becomes*! So everyone thinks everyone else has become the Thing! All *very* confusing! It becomes lots of the scientists but the other, 'un-Thinged' scientists find out who's real and who's a 'Thingummyblob' by testing their blood.

Well deserved doom The real scientists manage to destroy all the pretend 'Thinged' ones. Next, they drive the original 'Thing' out on to the ice. As it strikes at them with its snakelike fangs they blast it with blowtorches until it finally crawls away, its tentacles flailing and its flesh bubbling. Eventually it becomes a glowing lump. Ha ha ha!

Read all about it! In 'Who Goes There?' (1938) by J W Campbell.

Watch it! When you're old enough (and brave enough) in the film versions made in 1951 and 1982. The first version, made in black and white, is reckoned to be scarier than the bloodier remake. Rather than slinging gallons of gore, it hints at lots of hidden horrors and lets the viewer's imagination do its worst!

10 THE BLACK SPIDER

Appearance A huge, black, death-dealing spider with a difference.

Where found On the face of a woman who lives in a valley in Switzerland during the Middle Ages. Her friends are in danger from a band of cut-throats so she promises to give her baby to the Devil if he will save them. He snogs her to seal the deal. The woman just can't bring herself to hand over her nipper. This makes the Devil *really* angry so he takes his revenge. She begins to get a burning sensation in the place where he kissed her cheek. A spot appears which grows into a huge spider-shaped boil!

Behaviour The spider boil thingy gets bigger and bigger, then eventually bursts, releasing all the masses and masses of other spiders which have all been growing inside it! (For goodness sake, stop fiddling with that pimple, will you!) The spiders, which are the plague-carrying sort, scuttle off into the valley, spreading death and disease wherever they go!

Well deserved doom A man called Christian shouts at the big spider, has a scrap with it, then bungs it in a hole for ever. Hoorah! Everyone's happy, apart from Christian ... who's dead! Aaarh!

Read all about it! In 'The Black Spider' (1842) by Jeremias Gotthelf.

STORY 2: CAPTAIN MURDERER

Tale of terror number two is a story called 'Captain Murderer' (1860) by the mega-famous Victorian writer, Charles Dickens (1812–1870). You may find this one a bit hard to stomach. Because it's a very horrible and gruesome tale involving ... *cannibalism.*

Charles Dickens.

Charles said that he was first told this story by his nurse who got a 'fiendish enjoyment' from terrorizing him with it. He also said that she always began it by 'clawing the air with both hands and uttering a long low hollow groan'. Just the thing to lull the six-year-old, future author into a deep and tranquil sleep!

Charles recalled that the tale gave him his first ever shudder of terror and brought out cold beads of sweat on his forehead.

Would a modern nanny tell this story to the children she was looking after? Well maybe, if they were a really irritating pair of rug rats like the Torrington-Toasty twins. So let's bring the story up to date and see what happens!

ALL IN THE BEST POSSIBLE TASTE

It was night-time in the nursery and little Tim and Tabatha Torrington-Toasty were being tucked up in bed by their new nanny, Patience Dainty. Their rich and clever daddy, Tarquin Torrington-Toasty, was off on business in America and their even richer and cleverer mummy, Tara Torrington-Toasty, was off on a Caribbean island, writing a book on how to bring up children.

Once upon a time there was a very rich and handsome newspaper tycoon called Captain Murderer. He had a lovely house and lots of friends and a permanent suntan and everyone thought the world of him. When he passed people in his *fabulous* Mercedes motor car they would say, 'Oh, there goes Captain Murderer! What a *wonderful* man! So charming, so rich and so *successful*! Oh, if only *we* could be like *him*!'

Captain Murderer's favourite thing to do in all the world was getting married to nice ladies. Whenever he met a pretty woman who tickled his fancy he would ask her to marry him and she would usually say, 'Yes please!', what with him being so rich and handsome.

YOU'RE SO LOVELY I COULD EAT YOU!

OH... STOP BEING SILLY!

OH MY DEAR ... I'M DEADLY SERIOUS!

Then they would have a lovely wedding. The path to the church would be planted with pretty flowers and his new bride would say, 'Oh, what *strange* flowers! What are they?' and Captain Murderer would reply, 'They are the flavouring for the house-*lamb*, my dear!' Then he would laugh,

'Arrrf, arrf, arrf!' like that, and she would get to see his *very* sharp teeth for the very first time.

When Captain Murderer had been married to his tender young bride for one month and one day he would take out a trendy golden rolling pin and a snazzy silver pie-board and hand them to her. She would know exactly what they were for because, before they were married, Captain Murderer would have made sure she knew how to make pie crust. Next he would take out an enormous pie dish and lots of butter and flour and eggs, which of course, would be the ingredients for the pie crust. The only thing missing would be the pie filling itself.

Then she would look in the mirror and giggle dizzily, saying, 'But I can't *see* any meat!' And silly old Captain Murderer would laugh like a drain, frown like a rat, then whip out his huge, razor sharp, chef's knife and say, 'Now, get on with the crust at once, my dear! I'm *starving*!'

The moment the crust was ready Captain Murderer would cry, 'Look! There's the meat! It's in the mirror, now!' And his lovely young bride would run to the mirror and peer into it, just in time to see the Captain's chef's knife slashing at her pretty throat. (But at least she missed seeing her lovely head toppling from her shoulders and the blood gushing and geysering from the horrible ragged stump that used to be her neck.)

ARE YOU ENJOYING THE STORY, CHILDREN? YOU SEEM TO HAVE GONE EVER SO QUIET!

Slobbering noisily and licking his lips greedily, Captain Murderer would then fall to his knees and frenziedly slash and hack at his bride's still-twitching body until it was all chopped up into nice bite-size pie pieces. Next, he would cram the still warm 'bride-meat' into the pie dish, cover it in lots of salt and pepper and spicy herbs (or maybe even some garlic, chilli and parmesan cheese, if he fancied a change), slap on the crust and bung the whole lot into his gigantic oven. Then, as soon as it was cooked, he'd pig out on the absolutely scrumptious bride-pie for days on end, until, full up fit to bursting, he would sit by his blazing log fire, happily gnawing the last bits of meat from the bride-bones and letting out enormous burps and worse.

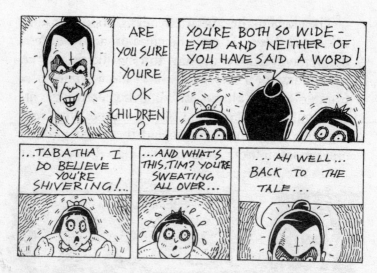

So this was how Captain Murderer passed his spare time. Meeting pretty ladies, marrying them ... then eating them! Hmmm ... yum yum! One day, Captain Murderer met the loveliest twin sisters he'd ever seen in his life. They were such a pair of smashers that he just couldn't make up his mind which one he should marry. The stunning blonde or the gorgeous dark-haired one? In the end he plumped for the dark-haired one because the blonde didn't fancy him one bit.

The blonde twin (who wasn't nearly as dim and trusting as her dark-haired sis') decided that there was something suspicious about her sister's new husband. So one day, crouching low to avoid the security sensors on the walls of his huge mansion, she snuck into his garden, climbed a convenient drainpipe and spied on him through his bathroom window. What a surprise she got! He was sitting in front of a great big mirror filing his teeth with an enormous file. It made a noise like this... *Rasp rasp rasp!* And every now and again he would spit out great mouthfuls of tooth.

At last his teeth were sharp like daggers and he left the bathroom.

Well, you know the rest. As usual, Captain Murderer put his wife to the knife. And all her sister could do was huddle in the garden listening to the heartbreaking screams, and the delighted roars of laughter from Captain Murderer ... 'ARRRF ARRRF ARRRF!' like that. There was no point in trying to rescue her. His house was *impossible* to get into! There was no point in calling the cops! They just wouldn't believe her. Everyone *loved* Captain Murderer.

It was around this time that the blonde twin decided that she would like to marry Captain Murderer too. So, one Saturday morning, while they were both in Sainsbury's, she just happened to knock her trolley into his and give him a very, very friendly wink. Within minutes he'd asked her to go out with him. Within weeks they were married. And before you could say, 'Sunday lunch!', there she was in his kitchen, rolling out the fatal pastry.

The Captain was as pleased as punch about marrying the second lovely twin but what he didn't know was this! Before she'd come to live with him, she'd made a special ingredient to give *her* pie crust some extra zest and zing. Her secret ingredient was hidden in a jar in the pocket of her apron. In it, all ground to a powder, were: rare and poisonous toadstools, rare and poisonous toads, vomit from a duck-billed platypus, and the diseased liver of a dying plague rat.

As Captain Murderer marched up and down the kitchen humming happily to himself, she craftily mixed the contents of the jar in with the pie-crust ingredients. Ten minutes later the crust was ready. Fifty minutes later, the blonde twin was beheaded by Captain Murderer and put in the pie. Well, she'd realized she'd have to make sacrifices.

Two hours later, Captain Murderer was shovelling down the pie, and thinking it was the very *best* he'd *ever* tasted. In fact, just as he was slurping the last of the scrummy marrow-jelly from the centre of his bride's thigh bone and mopping up the last of the bloody pie-juices with a chunk of that oh-so-tasty pie crust, he was feeling so good that he thought he'd go out to the local wine bar to chat to his famous friends.

Captain Murderer hadn't been in the wine bar long when he began to feel a little headachy, then a little dizzy, then a little sick. He thought he might just need to nip to the loo so he stood up, but immediately sat down again, because he'd noticed that his legs had gone numb and his stomach was swelling up faster than a frog that's sat on a foot-pump. As he clasped his hands to his rapidly expanding tum he noticed that they were turning blue and large red spots were beginning to appear all over them. It wasn't just his hands actually, it was his face and all the rest of him, which was probably why all the other people in the wine bar looked so shocked.

As Captain Murderer continued to inflate, horrible, extremely loud and extremely *rude* noises began to THWAAARRRRP and to THWEEEET from *all* the different holes of his body (including his ... *ears!*) and the whole wine bar was suddenly filled with the most revolting smells. Uuuurgh! When Captain Murderer had swollen up to the size of a small hot-air balloon the other celebrities finally realized that something might just be wrong. ('Puffed-up' types weren't unusual in the wine bar.) And just as Captain Murderer was thinking that if he got any bigger, he would burst ... he did.

There was the most *eeeeenormous* explosion ... KERPOW! ... and suddenly bits of Captain Murderer were flying in all directions. It was horrible to see! His bottom – yes, *just* his bottom – sailed across the wine bar and hit a top fashion designer in the face ... SPLATTT! ... just like that!

His intestine shot out of him like a spring-loaded trick snake, twizzled and twirled spectacularly in mid-air for a few moments, then wrapped itself around the neck of a well known pop singer. A famous soccer star was covered from head to toe with the entire (and extremely smelly) contents of his stomach.

One of his eyeballs ricocheted around the wine-bar walls like a demented pinball, then landed in the drink of a very famous, but very drunk, soap star who, mistaking it for a particularly interesting sort of olive, popped it into his mouth and swallowed it!

Oh, I can't go on, it's all too grisly and disgusting to tell! But, believe me, that really was the end ... of Captain Murderer!

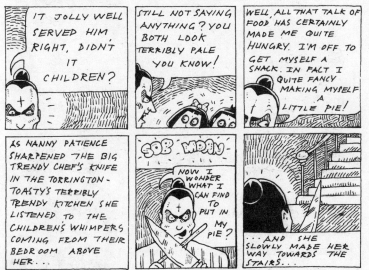

THE END

FANTASTIC FACTS 2: PREPARE TO MEET THEIR DOOM

Those poor women who were gobbled up by Captain Murderer are just a few of the many thousands of victims who've met their fates in all sorts of tales of doom and dreadfulness. Here's a list of six more horror victims and the loathsome bullies who made their lives (and deaths) a misery. After you've had a bash at matching the horrors to their screaming victims, check the answers to find out exactly who did what to whom ... and just *how* horribly they suffered (you *loathsome* little ghoul, you!).

HORRORS

1 Tiny men who appear as growths on human flesh and pull faces at their victim, bombarding them with non-stop chatter consisting almost entirely of unpleasant, hurtful and extremely personal remarks.

2 A mummified human head with cold, green staring eyes and long, snaky locks of black hair, sharp pointed teeth, and a leather skull-cap with 'ears'. The hideous great head is attached to a small shrivelled body all covered with dark curly hair.

3 Thousands and thousands (maybe even *millions*) of dirty great ants who are both ferocious and brainy (but not *that* brainy).

4 Red slime from a metal canister which has fallen to earth from space. It 'slithers' around the countryside, generally having fun and getting really big. (Imagine a huge dollop of extremely aggressive and energetic toothpaste rampaging up and down your high street.)

5 A huge ape that does horrendous things to its victim, then vanishes as if it had never existed.

6 A robot created by an old toy-maker as the 'perfect' dancing partner. It never puts a foot wrong, keeps perfect time and speaks as it dances, saying things like 'How charming you look tonight!' and 'I could go on dancing for ever.'

SCREAMERS

a) An inquisitive old farmer (bad tempered, smelly ... no one'll miss him), some 1950s teenagers (all quiffs and quarrels) and a few other unlucky types.

b) Annette, 'a bright, saucy little girl, fond of a frolic'.

c) An archaeologist called Dr Stokes who is excavating Inca burial mounds in Peru.

d) An explorer who disses a top African medicine man.

e) A famous doctor who goes on an archaeological dig in Egypt with his pal and steals some bones from a mummified body even though there is a chilling inscription on the tomb warning against such foolishness.

f) Another farmer. This one lives in Brazil and is brave, intelligent and plucky.

Answers:

1d) The victim is Stone in the story, 'Lukundoo' (1927) by EL White. Stone ends up covered in lumps. His pal slices off some of these 'carbuncles' but when he examines them carefully, to his horror, he realizes that they are not boils, but tiny human heads! He rushes to Stone just in time to see another hideous little man-thingy popping up out of the muscles of his chest! This one sticks out its tongue and squeaks insults at him, as its spindly little arms grab at Stone's beard.

His friend offers to give it the chop but Stone tells him that he is wasting his time as he is cursed for ever. Then he turns over and dies. It's the medicine man's horrible (but really witty) revenge! Spell available on request.

2c) The terrorizer and the terrorized meet in a story called 'The Flying Head' (1939) by A Hyatt Verrill. Despite warnings from his terrified Indian helpers, silly old Dr Stokes insists on removing the mummified head from its burial site and taking it back to his laboratory. (These crazy archaeologists *never* learn, do they.) During the night the thing comes to life, flaps those 'ears' on its leather helmet (yes, they're wings!), flies at Dr Stokes and rips out his throat.

3f) The victim is Leiningen in 'Leiningen versus the Ants' (1938) by Carl Stephenson. His farm is overrun by super-ants. The first he knows about them is a stampede of terrified animals rushing out of the jungle: pumas, jaguars, monkeys, etc., all fleeing the ant army. Next he sees a shapeless quivering thing that is black all over. It's a deer, entirely covered in ants which are biting it to death. Later in the story a similar thing happens to Leiningen. As the ants swarm all over him they bite him so badly that his body becomes one big open wound with the bones showing through. But at least he has anticipated them and set an anti-ant trap. As his farm workers pluck the ants from his body a combination of water and blazing petrol defeats the enemy!

He lives to farm another day. (But after that his life becomes one long anty-climax.)

4a) The terrorizer is 'The Blob', of course! From the 1958 movie of the same name. It sort of 'swallows' its victims then 'digests' them. The crusty old farmer gets *right* up its nose (or somewhere like that?) by poking his stick into the canister just moments after it's landed. Next moment... Slurrp! Buurpp!

The only thing that will destroy the Blob is the foamy stuff that comes out of fire extinguishers. And *you* thought they were for fires! The Blob! Coming to a classroom near you. Fire practice! *What* fire practice? This is *Blob* drill!

5e) The victim is Dr Morris from the story 'Monkeys' (1933) by EF Benson. The cursed mummy's tomb that he so foolishly stole from is guarded by menacing carvings of apes. As he sails back to England from Egypt, his servant hears screams coming from his cabin and rushes in to find that the doctor has been attacked by a giant ape which escapes through the window. All the ghastly things warned of on the tomb inscription have been done to him. His back is broken, handfuls of hair (with flaps of skin still attached ... uuurgh!) have been torn out of his head, his eyes have been 'scooped' out of their sockets and his thumb has been pulled out. Fancy him not heeding all those omens and warnings. Especially as they all stuck out like a sore thumb!

6b) The robot is the title-character of the story 'The Dancing Partner' (1893) by Jerome K Jerome. The toy-maker takes the robot to a dance where he attaches it to Annette's waist and starts them dancing. At first all is fine, but then the robot goes into overdrive, whirling Annette around the room faster and faster. It won't stop! People hurl themselves at the figure to try and disable it but this only makes matters worse and it begins smashing into walls and furniture.

By now Annette is injured and a trail of blood marks their crazy progress around the room. People rush off to find the toy-maker who's nipped off for a chat with the host. By the time he gets back it's too late! The author doesn't actually tell us that poor Annette is dead but, on entering the room, the host goes pale and says to all the other chaps, 'get the *women* away as quickly as you can' ... which sort of tells us she's been tango'd. (And that *he's* never heard of equality for women!)

STORY 3: WHILE ZOMBIES WALKED

No collection of horror stories would be complete without a story about the 'walking dead'. So tale number three is 'While Zombies Walked' (1939), a story by Thorp McClusky (1906–1975). The action takes place in America and the tale's what's known as a 'pulp fiction' horror story. In other words, it's not a classic horror story like *Dracula* or *Frankenstein* but it's a pacey and entertaining tale of terror with lots of thrills and action and a nice happy ending in which the baddies get what they deserve. Anthony, the story's young hero, will tell you all about it.

VOODOO SOMETHING TO ME

Let me introduce myself. My name's Kent, Anthony Kent. The story I'm gonna tell ya is an awful one. But it needs tellin'.

It all began when ma girlfriend, Eileen, dumped me back in the summer. Just wrote me this note:

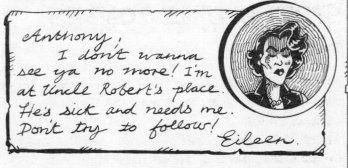

> Anthony,
>   I don't wanna see ya no more! I'm at Uncle Robert's place. He's sick and needs me. Don't try to follow!
>   Eileen.

'Crazy!' I thought. 'Only a month back she told me she loved me for always! There's somethin' real ... weeeeeeird ... goin' on here!'

I slung some stuff in ma old roadster and after three days hard drivin' I reached the hills where her uncle's place was. It was cotton-growing country with the sun beatin' down and guys workin' in the fields. As I cruised the dirt track I spotted a big old farmhouse on a hilltop up ahead a me. I stopped ma car and went over to a guy who was pullin' weeds.

'Scuse me, sir!' I said. 'Would that be the Perry place up yonder?'

But the guy just ignored me and carried on pullin' as if I wasn't there!

'Hey bud!' I said, 'I'm talkin' to you!' and grabbed his shoulder. As I did his hat fell sideways. And that's when I saw it. The top of the guy's head was smashed in! All bloody with jagged bone splinters pokin' every which way. An' worst of all ... there was a long grey ribbon of brain stuff hangin' down right next to his ear! I'm tellin' you ... he was gruesome! I let go of him like my fingers was burned and he went straight back to his weedin'! I jumped in ma car and raced to the farmhouse. There was an old fellah sittin' on the porch who fitted the description of Eileen's uncle.

'Mr Robert Perry?' I said.

He nodded, then said, 'You got a gun?'

'Mr Perry!' I said. 'There's a guy out there with his skull caved in. He's gonna die if he don't get help!'

'Die!' he laughed. 'He cain't never die!'

Just at that moment the biggest fellah I've ever seen comes out the door behind Mr Perry. He was wearing a preacher's outfit and had two other guys with him ... not quite so big ... but still, real big!

'This is the Reverend Barnes,' says Mr Perry. 'He's been ... "looking after" me.'

'Reverend Barnes!' I said. 'There's a guy working out in them fields. He's got a half a his head caved in and a piece a his brain's hangin' out 'longside his ear!'

'Nonsense!' laughed the big guy. 'Your brain's playin' tricks on you, boy. You've had too much sun, son.'

I started to wonder if he could be right. Just then I heard footsteps and suddenly Eileen was there looking beautiful as a plateful of black-eyed beans with hog-fried chitterlings!

'Eileen!' I blurted. 'I just had to come. I lurve ya, honey! What you doin' writin' me that goodbye note? You gone mad or sumpthin'?'

'Mad!' she laughed. 'No, Ant'ny, I ain't mad. No, not ... mad. It's just that I've ... I've ... I've ... changed! I don't never want to see you no more! Please ... go!'

But as she spoke her fingers traced a single word in the dust on the porch rail. I read it and as I did my lips musta said it without my brain knowin' because the next moment Reverend Barnes growled, 'What was that word you just said, boy?'

I said the word again and as I did the Reverend and his two goons jumped me! I didn't stand a chance. They clobbered me hard. Next thing I knew I was wakin' up in some sorta upstairs room in Mr Perry's farmhouse, tryin' for the life of me to remember that word what Eileen had wrote in the dust.

I looked outta the window. The sun was goin' down and a long line of men was trudgin' into the yard. It was the guys I'd seen workin' in the fields!

Some was draggin' their feet like they was doped. Others was a hobblin' an' a limpin' and a crawlin'. Man, they was a mess! One was no more 'n a hoppin' skeleton with just a withered arm and a stick leg. Another was a twitchin' an' jerkin' with a great swarm of flies a buzzin' and a crawlin' all over the strips of rotting yellow flesh that was danglin' offa him. And below the blank starin' eyes of another there was nothing but a big, mushy tangle-mangle of raw gristle an' stuff! He only had ... half a face! 'What the heck is going on here?' I thought. 'Ain't they got no worker's welfare union or nothin' at this pesky place!' And still, that word in the dust just wouldn't come back to me!

All of a sudden I heard noises in the room below. I dropped on all fours and peered through a crack in the floor. The Reverend was sittin' at a table while his goons were holdin' a scared lookin' guy up in front of him.

'You been a baaad boy!' yelled the Reverend. 'You're gonna suffffer for sleepin' on guard duty and lettin' that stranger in!' He waved a little doll thing at the guy and said, 'You know this here's made a your sweat and hair.'

The man looked terrified as the Reverend picked a fork off the table and jabbed it in the doll's leg. The guy screamed and went down on one knee. The Reverend jabbed the fork into the doll's middle part and the guy clutched his stomach and screamed some more. Over and over again, the Reverend stuck the fork in the doll. Jab! Jab! Jab! ... like that! And, as he did, the guy rolled around the floor, screechin' like a deep-fried bull frog. Then, all of a sudden, he went quiet.

'He's dead, boss!' said one of the goons. He was! I could see him laying there all stiff with his eyes wide and staring. And that Reverend hadn't touched him ... not once!

Right that moment I heard tapping on the wall next to me.

'Ant'ny! Ant'ny!' said a voice from the next room. 'You there? It's me, Eileen!'

'Eileen!' I said, putting my ear to the wall. 'What in reincarnation's goin' on?'

'It's the Reverend Barnes!' said Eileen. 'He's got us all in his power. But I wanted you to escape! That's why I wrote in the dust. I hoped you'd see it, then tell someone about the ... the ... the ... ZOMBIES!'

That was the word I'd been trying to think of! The one she'd written in the dust! Zombies! So that was what I'd seen in the fields. Those guys were the ... walkin' dead!

'Ant'ny, I do still lurve ya!' cried Eileen. 'The Reverend came here with his thugs and made a little doll of Uncle. Then he took one of the hairs offa his head and tied its legs up with it. That's why Uncle can't walk no more! The Reverend's took over the plantation and he's got his zombies working it. He's made a doll of me too and stuffed it with my hair! It was him that made me write you that note. He used to be a proper preacher but now he's a ... madman, Ant'ny!'

At that moment I heard the door to Eileen's room open and the sound of rough voices, followed by her scream of, 'Ant'ny! Help me! Help me!'

I hurled myself at my own door and beat my knuckles raw tryin' to get outta there and help her.

I could a saved myself the trouble though, because five minutes later the door opened and the thugs came in.

They dragged me outta there and down to a ginormous cellar full of giant wine barrels the size of small shacks. The Reverend was down there, standing next to Eileen who was sittin' in a chair. He was muttering some crazy-sounding words which I couldn't make out.

'What are you doing, you overgrown freak?' I yelled.

'I'm bindin' her with a voodoo magic spell!' snarled the Reverend. 'And soon, I'll do the same to you! Tie him up boys!'

The thugs did as they were told then sat at the Reverend's feet looking up at him like love-struck puppies. He reached into the big bag he'd got slung around his neck and pulled out two more dolls, just like the one I'd seen earlier. He began twisting and pulling them, and, as he did, the goons rolled around, moaning and twitching and gasping.

Their eyes almost popped outta their heads, their limbs jerked and stinky green vomit gushed outta their mouths like they was the twin Niagara Falls of puke! But after a while their twitching and jerking got less and less. Then, all of a sudden ... they were still!

'Oh shucks a'mighty!' I thought. 'If this madman destroys his own sort, what's he going to do to us?' and I began to struggle to free myself from the rope which held my wrists. I suddenly felt something sharp stick in me. It was a rusty nail poking out of the big wine barrel I'd been thrown against. I began to rub the rope on it, all the time keeping my eyes on the Reverend, who'd turned back to Eileen again.

'Ha ha ha!' he laughed crazily, rolling his bloodshot eyes

this way and that and dribbling all down the front of his nice clean cassock. 'I've never had a girlfriend as pretty as you before! Come to think of it, I've never even had a girlfriend! But now I got me one! Ha ha! I'm gonna put a spell on that boyfriend of yours — he's goin' to drive us to the city and get out all of his money from the bank and give it to me! Then, when I'm done with him I'll send him away in his car, stick a little pin in my doll and ... CRAAASH! That'll be the end of him. The doctors'll think he's had a heart attack! Ha ha ha!'

He reached into his bag and took out a needle and thread and some bits of cloth and began sewing. As he did, he mumbled some more of them strange-sounding words.

A few minutes later he'd got another one of the weird looking dolls in his hand. And it looked exactly like ... me!

'Now!' he said, walking towards me. 'Just a couple a strands!'

As he grabbed at my head, the nail I was rubbing on cut through the very last strand of the rope. In an instant I'd got my arms wrapped around the lunatic's legs and sunk my teeth into his thigh.

'Aaaaaagh!' he screamed and crashed down like a giant oak tree, sending dolls spinning every which way across the cellar floor. I leapt on top of him, punching and biting for all I was worth but, as I did, I felt those gigantic hands of his grab my neck. His strength was superhuman! No matter how I tore at his fingers I couldn't pull them off my throat. My windpipe felt like a ten-ton truck was parked on it! Stars swam before my eyes. But, just as I was about to plunge into blackness, I saw something sharp and glittery falling towards the Reverend's head. Next moment he let out a terrible scream and I saw his skull split open like a big juicy melon that's been sliced with a spade! Brains and blood spurted and splashed out of a gigantic gash that stretched from the bridge of his nose to the tip of his big greasy quiff! And as he slumped alongside me with the life a gushin' outta him I saw Mr Perry standing over him, holding a massive blood-stained axe and grinnin' fit to bust.

'Them pesky legs of mine!' he said, pointing to a little doll and a strand of thick grey hair just next to his feet. 'I got them sorted just in time. Hya hya hya!'

He'd hardly finished laughing when a great wailing and moaning began a comin' from the giant wine barrels. Next moment two shrivelled hands appeared over the edge of one. Then two more! Then more! Then a screaming head with empty sockets where the eyes shoulda been. Then a face with no mouth or nose. Dozens of zombies were pouring out of the wine barrels!

Eileen fell to the floor, sobbing in terror, her lovely eyes were huge pools of horror! Mr Perry grabbed the axe and put himself between her and the ghouls. The flesh on my back crawled and jiggered as I backed away from the gibbering corpses.

But we needn't have worried. The zombies weren't interested in us. They were seeking the peace of their graves. Now that the man who'd dragged them from their tombs and put that voodoo spell on them was dead, all they wanted was to return to their resting places. Five minutes later they'd all clambered up the cellar steps and their moans and wails were no more than the sound of distant wind.

'Oh Ant'ny, Ant'ny!' sobbed Eileen, when me and Mr Perry had finished burying the Reverend and his thugs. 'You were so brave. I'm sorry I wrote you that note.'

'Don't worry hon'!' I said, patting her gently on the head. 'These things happen.'

But she still wouldn't stop crying. So I planted a kiss on her quivering lips and she stopped right away. It worked like a charm. 'Magic!' I thought.

FANTASTIC FACTS 3: TEN FEARSOME FIENDS FROM AROUND THE WORLD

Do you think zombies really exist? Many people who live on the Caribbean island of Haiti still believe in them and are absolutely terrified of them. Most other people think they're just a sort of folk legend or story. For centuries people all over the world have been scaring each other stupid with tales of the horrible monsters that lurk in their local neighbourhood. Here are ten of the fearsomest fiends that have been frightening folk silly (or silly folk?) for absolutely ages.

1 ZOMBIES

Zombies are also known as the 'walking dead'. They can eat, hear and speak but can't remember anything from the past (and are therefore *completely useless* at spelling tests). It's said that evil magicians use a special sort of magic called 'voodoo' to turn people into zombies, either to make them into their slaves or to get revenge on them.

Here is one way in which a zombie is made. First of all a magician saddles his horse and rides it backwards to the victim's house. He then puts his lips to a slit in their front door and sucks out their soul (*sluuurrp* ... like that!) which he quickly spits into a bottle and traps with a cork. Just after this, the victim dies and is buried. The magician goes to their grave at midnight, opens it up and calls their name. Because he has got their soul, they sit up, and as they do he wafts the bottle under their nose. This brings them back to life (well, 'sort of') and they are then taken off to perform their zombie duties.

(All seems rather a lot of trouble just to get someone to do your ironing and cut your grass for you, doesn't it?) NB Please do not try this at home.

2 NUCKELAVEE

Nuckelavee has a head which is like a man's but at least ten times bigger. When he gets excited it rolls about so violently that it looks as if it's going to fall off. He hasn't got legs but his arms are so long they reach the ground. He has one red eye, a mouth like a pig's and his breath is so disgusting that it kills plants and makes animals sick. The most horrible thing about him is that he is *completely* skinless! He's covered in raw flesh that's covered with yellow veins all clotted with gungy black blood! You're most likely to bump into him in Scottish folk tales.

67

3 SWEENEY TODD

Sweeney Todd was a barber in Victorian London (or so they say!). Whenever a likely looking customer sat in his barber's chair, Sweeney would nip into the back room of his shop, pull a lever and the chair would tip backwards, pitching the victim through a trapdoor and into the cellar. Sweeney would then trot downstairs and chop them up into little pieces so that Mrs Lovett at the pie shop next door could put them in her famous, extra tasty, meat pies. The closest shave you're likely to get with Sweeney is in the Victorian version of pulp fiction known as Penny Dreadfuls.

4 BLACK ANNIS

Black Annis was a horrible hag who lived in a cave in Leicestershire. She had one eye, a red face and long curving claws. She would crouch in the branches of an oak tree at twilight, waiting for children to pass. When they did, she'd pounce on them and skin them alive, using those horrible claws of hers. After she'd eaten their flesh she'd add their hide to her collection of children's skins which she proudly displayed on the walls of her cave (a bit like other people display their best china or football posters). Her cave and oak tree were probably flattened to make way for a motorway service area absolutely ages ago, so your chances of bumping into her are very slim.

5 SPRINGHEEL JACK

Springheel Jack bounced around the streets of Victorian London terrorizing women all over the place. He was said to have eyes like balls of white fire, horns like a goat, wings like a bat and a long tail. When he attacked he would vomit blue and white flames at his victims and scratch them with his long metal claws. If you did bump into him he'd probably be gone in a flash as he was especially good at jumping over really high walls. Probably a mate of Sweeney Todd's!

6 THE SASQUATCH

Sasquatch is a Native American Indian word which means Hairy Giant. When the white settlers arrived in North America and found out about the Sasquatch they decided to name this huge gorilla-like creature Bigfoot, because it left big footprints wherever it went. There are lots of stories about the Sasquatch, including one told by a lumberjack who said he was kidnapped by a family of Sasquatch who kept him as a pet (but were forced to let him go when the vet's bills got too much). A similar creature to the Sasquatch is the Yeti which is reported to have been seen in the Himalayas (though it might just have been a Sasquatch on its hols). In 1918, the *Seattle Times* confidently reported that Bigfeet were 8 feet tall, 'half-human half-monster', could hypnotize people, throw their voices *and* make themselves *invisible* whenever they wanted to! So there's no point in going looking for them, is there?

7 BANSHEES

A banshee is a horrible female spectre that is always groaning and wailing. It has one nostril, a huge sticky-out front tooth, webbed feet and eyes that are red from constant crying. It's said that the wail of the banshee warns that a death is about to take place. If you hear lots of banshees wailing together it means that a holy person is going to die (or they're all trapped in a wailway station). You might bump into a banshee in Ireland, or if you're very unlucky, in Scotland, where they can sometimes be seen washing bloodstained clothes in rivers (but hardly ever at the local laundrette).

8 CURUPIRA

Curupira lives in the deepest, darkest, most mysterious part of the Amazon jungle. He's easy to recognize because he's short and hairy and his feet are on back to front! You won't have any trouble bumping into him either! He'll find *you*! This spooky South American bogey beast is a child-catcher who'll call you to him with a whistling sound that you just won't be able to resist. After that he'll take you into the deepest, darkest bit of the forest and you'll never be seen again – except by Curupira, of course!

9 TROLLS

Trolls have got bulging eyes, long mega-powerful arms, swollen noses and are covered all over in earth and moss. They walk around with their mouths open and drool a lot. During the daytime they stay in their caves but in the evenings they love to go out clubbing ... humans to death, so they can eat them. At one time, Norway used to be absolutely teeming with trolls.

10 THE NIGHT HAGS

The little babies and toddlers of old days Eastern Europe didn't have Telly Tubbies to keep them amused. They had Night Hags! If their mums had forgotten to bless them at bedtime the Hags would come to the children during the night and do whatever they could to make them cry, including prodding them, and even sucking the blood from their veins!

The Night Hag of Bulgaria was definitely the worst of the lot. This horrendous thing, which had the body of a woman and the head of an ox, would crawl into the child's bedroom, then hang over their cot, just *breathing* on them. A few days later the poor child would die of some horrible illness! (And you thought Tinky Winky was a pain!)

STORY 4: THE MONKEY'S PAW

The fourth tale in our tremblesome Ten Best is the story called 'The Monkey's Paw' (1902) by WW Jacobs (1863–1943). Unlike most horror stories there aren't any over-the-top descriptions of gruesome gore in it. The action takes place in the sort of ordinary and comfortable family home that most people live in so when the horror eventually does arrive it somehow seems extra terrifying. The writer slowly builds up the spine-chilling atmosphere, then finally just sort of 'suggests' the hideous thing that may be out there. The rest is left to the reader's imagination! This extremely scary, but rather sad story, with its simple and clever plot, is perfect for turning into a stage play. No special effects are needed ... just lots of good acting and directing. Maybe you could get together with some talented pals and make it the school drama production that frightens the life out of the other kids and teachers?

THE GOOD LUCK CURSE

Scene One: *The cosy sitting-room of a family home somewhere in the south of England. A father and his grown-up son are playing chess. On the other side of the room a woman is knitting and casting loving glances at the happy pair. A cheery fire blazes in the hearth. A feeling of warmth and family togetherness fills the room.*

Mr White: (*glancing at clock*) He's late. I'm sure he should have got here by now.
The front door bell rings.
Mrs White: Ah! That'll be him now. I'll put the kettle on.
Mr and Mrs White leave the room. Moments later Mr White re-enters with a man in army uniform.

Mr White: Herbert, I'd like you to meet Sergeant-Major Morris. We go back a long way. In fact, when he left the warehouse to serve in India, we were both lads!
Herbert: Pleased to meet you, Sergeant-Major.

Mrs White: (*entering with tray*) Tea's up, chaps!
Mr White: Now, Morris, tell us all about India.

Scene Two: *The same sitting-room an hour later.*

Mr White: Well, you've certainly had some adventures, Morris. What was that story you were telling me the other day? About a monkey's paw or something?
Sergeant-Major Morris: Oh that's nothing...
Mrs White: (*intrigued*) A monkey's paw?
Sergeant-Major Morris: Well, it's just a bit of magic or what have you. It's nothing to look at...
He fumbles in his pocket. The family lean forward as he holds something out in the palm of his hand. It's the paw of a monkey, dried like a mummy. Mrs White looks rather disgusted but Herbert takes the paw and studies it with interest.

Mr White: So, what's so special about it then, Morris?
Sergeant-Major Morris: It had a spell put on it by an Indian fakir a long time ago. He wanted to show that everyone's life is ruled by fate. He reckoned our futures are planned out for us and that anybody who tries to

interfere with their fate only brings sorrow on themselves.

Herbert: Sort of ... what will be, will be! No matter what!

Sergeant-Major Morris: That's right, Herbert. The fakir put a spell on the paw so that three separate people could each have three separate wishes from it.

Mr White: Well, why don't you have three then, Morris?

Sergeant-Major Morris: (*hesitantly, almost in a whisper*) I have. I'd prefer not to talk about them if it's all the same to you.

Mrs White: And who else has had the wishes?

Sergeant-Major Morris: (*still subdued*) Just one other man. The one who had it before me. His last wish was for death. That's how I got the paw.

Without warning, he throws the paw on to the fire but Mr White reaches down and snatches it off again, just as quickly.

Sergeant-Major Morris: Let it burn.

Mr White: Seems a waste not to use the last three wishes.

Sergeant-Major Morris: Well, if you keep it and use it, don't blame me for what happens.

Mr White: Tell us! How do you make the wish?

Sergeant-Major Morris: Hold it up in your right hand and say your wish out loud. But I'd advise you to get rid of it. Don't say I didn't warn you!

Scene Three: *Same room an hour later. The Sergeant-Major has departed.*

Mrs White: Well that was a nice evening. That Sergeant-Major Morris certainly can spin a good yarn.

Herbert: If the story about the paw is as far-fetched as his other tales I reckon you're going to be disappointed! Ha ha!

Mrs White: Anyway dear, what are you going to wish for?

Mr White: To be honest with you I can't think of anything. I've got all I could ever want. The love of a good wife, my job, my health. And of course, the most wonderful son anyone could ever wish for.

Herbert: So where does *he* live then, Dad? Ha, ha, ha! Seriously though. What about paying off the mortgage on our house? Surely that would make you happy. Why don't you wish for two hundred pounds?

Mr White: (*holding paw up*) Good idea, our Herbert! All right then! I wish for two hundred pounds. Aaaargh!

Mrs White: What's the matter? What's the matter?

Mr White: It moved in my hand. The paw! As I made the wish. It wriggled ... just like a lizard!

Herbert: I think your imagination is getting the better of you, Dad!

Mr White: Yes, maybe it is. Anyway, there's no harm done.

Scene Four: *The next morning. The kitchen of the White's home. They are sitting round the breakfast table.*

Mrs White: Well, we didn't wake up to find a bag of money under the bed, did we? What a load of nonsense that soldier talked! And more to the point, if the wish had come true, how could getting two hundred pounds hurt us?

Herbert: It might fall on our heads from the sky. Ha ha! Anyway I must be off now or I'll be late for work!

Mr White: Bye, son. Take care.

Mrs White: See you tonight, love. Ta ta!

She kisses Herbert and he leaves.

Scene Five: *The same day. Late afternoon. Mr and Mrs White are drinking tea in the front room.*

Mrs White: Still no sign of that two hundred pounds then. Ha ha!

Mr White: I knew that paw business was a load of tosh! I suppose our Herbert will have something funny to say about it when he gets in!

As he speaks, Mrs White gets up and goes over to the window.

Mrs White: Ooh! There's a chap at our front gate. He's looking at the house and checking a bit of paper. He's very smart and official-looking. Like he's from a bank or somewhere?

Mr White: Hmm, wonder what he wants?

Mrs White: He's coming up our path. You don't think it could have anything to do with your wish for two hundred pounds, do you?

Mr White: I don't know. Let's let him in and find out!

Mrs White goes to the door and moments later she re-enters with the stranger.

Mrs White: Have a seat, sir.

Stranger: I'd rather stand, if you don't mind. Mr and Mrs White, I've got some news for you. I'm here from Meggins and Maw. It's not good news, I'm afraid. There's been an accident. At the factory. Your son's been hurt.

Mrs White: Oh my goodness gracious! My poor lad! Is he hurt bad?

Stranger: Very, very bad. But he's not in pain. Not any more...

Mr White: Do you mean...?

He claps his hand to his mouth while Mrs White begins to weep uncontrollably.

Stranger: Yes, I'm afraid to say that ... he's dead. Somehow, he got caught up in the pulping machine. No one knew he was in there for a while, what with the noise drowning out his screams. By the time we switched off the power, it was too late.

Mr White: Oh my poor, poor boy.

Stranger: The firm has instructed me to inform you that they'd like to offer you compensation for your loss. We will give you the sum of ... two hundred pounds.

Mrs White: Oh no! Oh no! Oh no!

She begins to shriek uncontrollably and tear wildly at her hair. Mr White slumps to the floor in a dead faint.

Scene Six: *Some days later. The White's semi-darkened bedroom. Mr White is in bed but Mrs White is standing at the window peering up the street.*

Mr White: What are you doing, love? There's no point looking for him. He ain't coming back. Come to bed right now or you'll get cold.

Mrs White: Not as cold as my poor son.

He turns over and appears to go to sleep. Some moments pass then Mrs White suddenly seizes Mr White by the shoulder and shakes him violently.

Mrs White: Wake up! Wake up! The paw! Where is it?

Mr White: Hmmph! Why? What's the matter?

Mrs White: We've got two more wishes left! We only used one! Oh, why didn't I think of it before? We had the first one granted, didn't we? So why can't we make a second?

Mr White: (*now out of bed*) I don't think we ought to do that! I really don't...

Mrs White: But of course we should! Get the paw! Now!

Mr White: Listen, love. We don't know what the horrid thing will do...

Mrs White: We've got to take a chance... We've got to get our son back.

Mr White gets out of bed and exits as Mrs White frantically paces the bedroom. After a few seconds he returns with the paw.

Mr White: I really do not think...

Mrs White: Wish!

Mr White: But...

Mrs White: WISH!

Mr White: (*raising the paw*) I wish to see my son alive once more.

He drops the paw and sits on the bed. Mrs White rushes over to the window. They remain like this for some moments then she joins him and they both stare at the floor. A few more moments pass then a slow knocking begins to sound below them. At first they hardly hear it but then…

Mrs White: Listen. What is that?

Mr White: (*beginning to tremble*) It's nothing. Just a branch in the wind or something.

The knocking gets louder.

Mrs White: It's him! Herbert! He's come back. Oh, Herbert ... my Herbert! I must let him in.

She leaps to her feet but Mr White grasps her by the arm.

Mr White: No, don't! Don't let it in! Please, please ... don't!

Mrs White: Are you afraid of ... your own son?

Mr White: (*almost hysterical*) Don't let it in! PLEASE ... DON'T LET IT IN!

The knocking is getting louder than ever now.

Mrs White: (*pushing her husband aside*) I'm coming, Herbert! I'm coming!

She rushes from the room. The knocking is frantic now and reverberates around the house. Mr White sits on the bed shuddering all over. Down below a bolt is heard to slide.

Mrs White: The top bolt. I can't reach it. Help me! Help me!

The knocking gets even wilder. Mr White falls to his knees and scrabbles around on the floor. He finds something and holds it above his head. It's the paw.

Mr White: Please! Please let it die once more. Let it be gone ... for ever!

The knocking stops. There's the sound of a chair being dragged across the floor, a second bolt being pulled and a door opening. Mrs White is heard to scream. She returns to the bedroom ... alone and ashen faced.

FANTASTIC FACTS 4: NO NEED TO BE AFRAID

Poor old Mr White! He was completely overcome with his fear of what might be on the other side of that door, wasn't he? Fear really is a strange thing. Why do we get it? Does it smell? Can it be good for you? To find out, we tuned in to a local radio 'Fear Special'...

CALL STU PIDTWERP! A RADIO MOAN-IN

Tonight's question: 'Fear! What actually is it?'
Special guest: Professor Tim Idwimp

Hi, all you 'fraidy cats out there! Stu Pidtwerp here! I've got Tim Idwimp with me. He's an expert on all things scary and he's here to answer your questions about fear. Please make allowances for him, he's not been on radio before, so he's a bit nervous. Here's our first caller. She's Lily Livered from Crouch End.

Hello, T-Tim. Could you t-tell me w-w-why w-we f-feel f-fear?

W-w-well Lily, if w-we d-didn't, we probably w-w-wouldn't be around for l-long.

You mean it helps us survive everyday dangers, Tim?

Yes! If we didn't f-feel fear we might be out w-walking in the p-park when round the corner comes a runaway horse and next m-moment…

KERRPOWW!

Aaagh!

STU

Sorry Tim, didn't mean to frighten you like that! Let me help you back into your chair. Now … what were you saying?

W-well, in an emergency like the one with the runaway horse, if our f-fear reactions didn't take over immediately, we'd just stand there l-like a lemon and…

…get turned into squash? Ha ha!

Exactly! So w-what I'm trying to say is that fear can b-be r-really useful.

Brilliant! Next caller please. It's Wayne Widdle from Great Piddling-In-The-Bog.

Hi Tim, what actually happens to our bodies when we get frightened?

All sorts really. But the main reactions are: a) your heart begins to beat f-f-faster b) the pupils of your eyes get b-bigger c) fuel is delivered to your muscles very quickly ... and d) you f-feel a desperate need to visit the toilet, Wayne. All these things are our body's way of preparing itself to run away from whatever we're afraid of ... or to do battle with it. We call it the 'flight or fight' reaction.

Fascinating! Next question please, from Mr Willy Chickenout.

Why do we get goosebumps when we're frightened, Tim?

Many experts b-b-believe they're a leftover from prehistoric t-t-times when we were all covered in hair. If a fearsome enemy approached, our hair would automatically stand on end, making us look much b-b-bigger than we really were.

Hey! That's exactly what my cat does whenever I go near it!

Even though w-we've no longer got as much b-b-body hair as w-we used to have we've still got the little root b-b-bumps it stood in. They don't seem to have realized that things have changed so they carry on standing to attention whenever we're afraid.

Well I'll be jiggered! OK ... our next caller is Miss Emma Fraidalot.

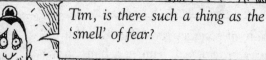

Tim, is there such a thing as the 'smell' of fear?

Yes there is, Emma. When an animal senses d-danger its b-b-body leaks out smelly chemicals called pheremones which warn its pals that there's trouble about. We're still not entirely sure whether this h-happens in h-humans.

Amazing! Right, next caller please. It's a Ruth Lessmonster from Hackney.

Tim! What's the big deal with scary horror stories?

People have been, er, enjoying horror stories for hundreds of years. They're b-b-both enjoyable and useful. For example, in the old days p-people would tell them to their children to let them know about the d-d-dangers that lurked in the forests. So the children would be educated and entertained at the same time.

Sort of edu'tainment? Ha ha. But why are horror stories and films so incredibly popular nowadays, Tim?

Well, when p-people read horror stories or watch horror films they experience all the f-fear reactions we were talking about earlier. The b-big b-b-buzz they get from the 'flight or fight' feeling makes them feel extra zingy and alive all over.

Sort of chilled ... but thrilled?!

Yes. And deep down they know they've nothing to fear because it's all make-believe. It's like having a really b-bad n-nightmare but knowing you can wake up from it whenever you feel like it.

Yeah! You're chilled and thrilled ... but not killed! Ha ha! OK, I'm afraid – ha ha ha! – that it's time to take a short commercial break now! Join us again in a while!

Er, Stu!? D-d-do you think you could tell me where the little boy's room is? I'm d-dying for a w-w-wee-wee...

Shut up, Tim! We're still on air...

STORY 5: THE PIT AND THE PENDULUM

Have you got a fear of being trapped all on your own in a *very* small place? Perhaps in a lift, or in the school dungeon. (Don't say you didn't know about *that*.) If you have, you'd better not read the story that's been sort of '*squeeezed*' into the number five slot here. It's 'The Pit and the Pendulum' (1842) by Edgar Allan Poe (1809–1849). Edgar was a master horror writer who is famous for lots of other tales of terror, including 'The Masque of the Red Death' and 'The Fall of the House of Usher'. He was especially fond of dreaming up stories about people being buried alive. In this tale of terror a man is tried and sentenced to death. The cell that he's put into

Edgar Allan Poe.

is a most 'interesting' room with many utterly horrendous features. His deeply uncomfortable dungeon would make a great subject for one of those 'room of my own' type features that glossy magazines are so fond of.

IT'S THE PITS!

A Room To Die ~~For~~ In!

Our roving interior style reporter, Vic Tim, pays a visit to a unique basement room and gets an insider's view of just how the Spanish Inquisition achieve that ever so trendy and sought after 'distressed' look.

Hi! This month I've been to a castle in southern Europe and taken an 'in-depth' peep at a very unusual cellar conversion. I didn't really choose the room myself. I just sort of ended up there. How did I get there? Well, as you probably know, there's been a lot of unpleasantness in that part of the world just lately. There's been a rather messy little war going on. And that horrible mob who call themselves the Inquisition have been up to their old tricks! Sticking their noses into other folks' business and doing horrible things to them. And guess what! Silly-old-me got arrested by them and put on trial for this, that and the other. Oooh ... that courtroom! Talk about 'tacky'!

THE COURTROOM: *They tried. But in my judgement ... it was a case of design disaster!*

Uurgh! Those walls! Naff's not in it. They were sort of black and furry, with a weird rippling effect. Evidence enough for me to realize that this lot were guilty of criminal bad taste. What with the wibbly walls, the flickering candles and the murmuring of the judges I eventually fainted. I suspect that hearing them pass the death sentence on me may have also had something to do with that!

MY CELL: *Compact, very compact. With wall-to-wall, er ... walls!*

When I came to, I hadn't the faintest idea where I was! 'Uh oh!' I thought. 'I don't think I'm going to like this one bit!' I mean, I'm fond of subdued lighting, but this was ridiculous. It was pitch black. I couldn't see my nose in front of my face. In a moment of mad panic, I thrashed my arms about, felt nothing ... and breathed a sigh of relief. Well, at least I hadn't been buried alive! Believe me, I like cosy, but to discover that I'd been banged up in a coffin really would be the death of me! 'Time to check out the accommodation!' I thought. I stood up and began to inch my way forwards, hands outstretched. After a good few steps, I touched something. It was a wall. It could have been stone. But its

surface felt very smooth, very cold and very slimy! 'Uuurgh!' I thought. 'Whatever that is, it's certainly not going to replace cork tiles or corrugated coconut as this year's favourite wall covering!' I followed the wall for a while then stopped and began to make my way back to my starting point. All of a sudden I slipped in the disgusting layer of crud and gunge on the floor. (Haven't this lot heard of carpets?) 'Ah well!' I thought, 'I'm down in the ooze, so I might as well snooze.'

THE EN-SUITE PIT: *A 'deeply' stylish centrepiece ... and 'well' trendy! Only recommended for home decorators who are prepared to take the plunge!*

Some time later I awoke. 'Time for more walkies!' I thought, as I climbed out of my sleeping-bog. 'I've done the walls so I'll check out the centre this time.' I hadn't gone far when I got my feet tangled up and I fell flat on my face. Ouch! As I lay there recovering, I realized that my chin was resting on the floor but the rest of my face wasn't! 'Odd!' I thought. 'Why is the top half of my mush dangling in space? And what's that dreadful pong? It's sort of 'toilety' ... with a hint of rotting cabbage and a whiff of damp hamster! And why does the air feel so clammy all of a sudden?' Carefully, I stuck out my arm and had a feel around. Nothing! I realized my face was hanging over a hole! I managed to dislodge a stone from its rim and let it drop. After what seemed like ages, I heard a splash as it hit water. So that was it! They'd given me my own en-suite PIT! How thoughtful of them. The little tinkers had been hoping I'd go blundering about in the pitch dark and topple right into it. Oooh! The depths some people will sink to. As carefully as I could, I backed away from the pit, hoping there weren't any more. When I thought I was well clear, I got down on the floor, curled up, and slept for what must have been hours. My little adventure had exhausted me!

WACKY 'IRON-IC' MURALS: *Designed to drive you completely up the wall!*

When I finally awoke, my prison was lit by a dim glow. At last I could get a proper look at it! Well, it wasn't nearly as big as I'd thought. And the walls weren't stone! They were made from huge metal panels which were covered all over with really scary paintings. Demons and skeletons, people having their insides pulled out with giant pincers, giants biting the heads off babies, men with their brains squirting out of their ears ... fun stuff like that! Some people have the weirdest taste in art, don't they? I'm more of a soothing sunset or cute kitten person myself.

AND SO TO BED! *Stylish and comfortable – well, at a stretch – and certainly very ... 'restrained'!*

It wasn't too easy checking out the decor because I was now stretched out on some sort of wooden frame. A bit like one of those Japanese 'futon' beds. Yes! Very trendy. But very painful too! While I'd been off in the land of nod my new 'chums' had strapped me down, leaving only my head and my left arm free.

THE DINING AREA: *With an irresistible flavour of the Mediterranean!*

They'd left my arm free so I could just reach the plate of meat that was next to me. I was starving so I grabbed a huge piece and gobbled it down! Uuurgh! Was it salty! They must have smothered it with the entire contents of the Mediterranean Sea! I reached for the water jug. But of course! It was empty, wasn't it! The things people will do to make the last moments of your life completely unbearable. Sometimes I really could ... SCREAM!

THE FEATURE CEILING: *Highly original ... but soooo over the top!* Anyway, as I didn't have to rush off anywhere, I thought I'd pass the next decade or three gazing at the ceiling. It was at least 10 metres above me and made of metal, just like the walls. They were obviously trying to achieve the 'co-ordinated look' that's all the rage in torture chambers this season. Staring down at me was an ancient chap with a long white beard. Old Father Time himself. Not the real one! Just a painting. But still, very spooky! Sticking out of the painting was his scythe. Well, it wasn't so much a scythe as a dirty great pendulum thingy. Like a big brass rod with some sort of weight on the end. And it was moving! Backwards and forwards. Backwards and forwards. Normally I might have found this quite relaxing – but not this time! Especially when I noticed that the 'weight' was an extremely large and sharp blade which appeared to drop a fraction lower at every swing. If I had to be mesmerized by anything I would have much preferred a soothing lava lamp with its globs of oil bobbling about. Or even a tank of tropical fish!

A REMOTE, RESTFUL REFUGE FROM THE RAT RACE?
But then I meet the neighbours!

As I lay there gawping up at the razor-edged blade and thinking, 'By Ikea! If that thing ever reaches my rib cage, my chest is going to look like an explosion in a giblets factory!' I was suddenly distracted by a squeaking noise coming from the direction of my en-suite pit. I glanced across and was horrified to see hundreds and hundreds of enormous rats scrambling out of it and heading towards me! They were great fat things, the size of Dobermann puppies! All with eyes like blazing match-heads and teeth like kebab skewers! It was meat they were after. Mine! 'No way!' I thought 'This is my body and that's my din-dins. Salt or no salt!' I began to bat them away with my free hand. I don't know how long I'd spent beating off the charge of the bubonic brigade when I happened to glance up at the pendulum again. It seemed to have descended at least another 3 centimetres. 'Uh oh!' I thought. 'Now I really am in trouble! I know I'm definitely not imagining things now. If that thing keeps descending at this rate my most important and favourite internal organs are going to be minced morsels before I'm much older!'

HOME SWEET HOME: *So, just how 'distressed' can one get?!*

Well, the days went by with me passing my time watching that horrible blade getting closer and closer, fighting off the hairy hordes that kept pouring out of the pit, and generally being permanently scared out of my skull! I really hadn't realized that it was possible to scream so long and so loud without actually pausing for breath. At last it got to the point where that glistening razor edge was swishing backwards and forwards just millimetres from my quivering ribs. 'I've got to do something!' I thought. 'I can't just lay here and let it happen!'

That was when my great idea hit me. It was brilliant! Or so I thought at the time. I reached out and grabbed the very last bit of meat from the dish and began rubbing it on the straps that held me down. Then, with a cheery cry of, 'Come and get it chaps! It's your favourite: beef-flavoured fetters, all drenched in tangy human sweat!' I lay very, very still. At first the rats were suspicious. But then the smell of nosh became too much for them. And they were on me like a shot!

Listen, bonding with our animal chums is all well and good! Taking the dog for a walk. Pony riding. Swimming with dolphins. All fine. But when it comes to rats don't even think of it! This was sheer TORTURE! They were everywhere. And I do mean everywhere! On my face. In my hair. Up my robe! You name it ... they stuck their noses in it! They were into every nook and cranny I'd got. Not to mention some I didn't know I'd got!

97

Nevertheless, I lay there not moving a muscle and thinking that sooner or later I'd be free. And it worked! They nibbled and nibbled and eventually the straps fell away. Yahoo! With an almighty effort I pulled myself up, sending rats flying in all directions. 'Ha, ha ... ya suckers!' I thought, looking up at the ceiling behind which I guessed my hosts were lurking. 'I bet you didn't think of that!' But they had. Of course they had! They'd thought of everything. At that moment the pendulum stopped swinging. And seconds later it was pulled up through a hole in the roof. They'd been watching me all the time! The good for nothing so-and-sos had dreamed all this up just to amuse themselves. They were in complete control of everything that was happening to me. I was nothing more than their plaything!

FINISHING TOUCHES: *How to create that really warm and intimate feel.*

I was on the point of yelling, 'Just leave me alone will you, you vicious monsters?' and 'Why don't you do what all the other pompous, power-crazed morons in the world do? Yes, why don't you take up ... golf!' when I noticed that my room was getting warmer. Not, 'Ooh, isn't it chilly, let's turn up the central heating a few notches' warmer, but, 'this should have that whole ox-carcass roasted in no time' warmer! In fact, as I felt the heat blisters beginning to form on my feet I saw that the metal panels of the walls were actually beginning to glow! And at the same time, something else was happening. My room was shrinking! Rapidly! In a matter of minutes it was half its original size. The panels, which were now white hot, were closing in on me from all sides. As they did I was driven to the brink of the pit. 'So this is The End!' I thought. The deadly dungeon-designer's party piece! The fatal finishing touch! Then, as I teetered on the brink of the pit wondering which would be the least painful way to die: to be fried to death in a white-hot metal coffin or to fall into a pit and be gnawed to death by rampant rodents, I heard the sound of trumpets and excited human voices from somewhere above me. At that point I fainted and plunged towards the abyss!

THE TABLES ARE TURNED: *I get to see ... some 'general' improvements!*

That was all a couple of weeks ago. And I'm pleased to say that things have changed a lot since then. Just as I was on the point of toppling into the abyss I felt strong arms pull me to safety. They belonged to the general of the army that had just overthrown the Inquisition. It was their victorious trumpets I'd heard just moments before. So I lived to tell the tale. And now I'm looking forward to a change of rooms! So don't forget to check out my column in the 'Fall' issue of Wicked Interiors. The editor's sending me off to 'The House of Usher' ... wherever that is!? One thing's for sure, it just can't be worse than that dismal dungeon!

FANTASTIC FACTS 5: SPOT THAT PHOBIA!

That fear of being trapped in a very small space (like a coffin) which Edgar's character suffered from, is known as claustrophobia. Quite a few people seem to have their own little phobias. The most common ones are things like the fear of heights, the fear of dogs, the fear of flying, fear of the dark and the fear of creepy-crawlies. Makers of horror movies and writers of certain sorts of horror books make the most of these exaggerated fears in order to get their audience and readers all of a tremble. If you haven't already got a phobia of your own ... don't worry! There are absolutely *hundreds* to choose from! If you were *really* desperate you could even have '*fear of never suffering from a phobia*' phobia!

Let's rejoin Stu Pidtwerp and his guest and find out a bit more.

CALL STU PIDTWERP! A RADIO MOAN-IN

Hello again listeners! Welcome back to our fear special. I've got a Mr Ivor Dreadov on the line. He wants to know all about phobias!

Tim, what's the difference between a fear and a phobia?

Well, Ivor. A fear's a n-normal and n-natural reaction to danger but a phobia's a sort of over-the-top and unnecessary reaction. It's like the b-body's warning system has gone all haywire with the alarm bells ringing even when there's really n-n-nothing to be afraid of!

I've a dread of...

Yes?

Shut up Ivor, I'm not talking to you! I was about to say that, I've a dread of ... creepy-crawlies. Especially greenfly! I go to pieces when I see one!

Yes Stu! I know w-what you mean. My own p-p-personal phobia is a terror of people scraping their teeth with their fingernails.

What! Like this?
Scrape scrape scrape scrape...

Aaagh! Aaagh! D-don't d-do it! Let m-me out, let m-me out, l-let m-m-me out!

Come back, Tim! Come back! Oh dear, listeners, I'm 'afraid' Tim's run out on us! Ha ha ha! But don't worry because it's time to play 'Spot That Phobia!' All you have to do is match the word to the fear. Oh cripes … is that a … greenfly?

1 Is **pantophobia...**
a) a fear of underwear
b) a fear of everything
c) a fear of getting out of breath?

2 Is **bogyphobia...**
a) a fear of going to the toilet
b) a fear of demons and goblins
c) a fear of all that gungy stuff you find up your nose?

3 If you had **brontophobia** would you have...
a) a fear of thunder storms
b) a fear of Victorian women writers
c) a fear of dinosaurs?

4 Is **arachibutyrophobia...**
a) a fear of spiders
b) a fear of itching
c) a fear of getting peanut
butter stuck to the roof of
your mouth?

5 Is **gymnophobia...**
a) fear of exercise
b) fear of nudity
c) fear of gymnasiums?

6 If you had **batophobia**
would you be suffering from...
a) a fear of cricket equipment
b) a fear of nocturnal flying
mammals
c) a fear of high buildings?

7 Is **polyphobia...**
a) the fear of colleges
b) the fear of parrots
c) the fear of many things?

8 Does someone with
hagiophobia have...
a) a fear of witches
b) a fear of bargaining
c) a fear of saints?

9 Is **spectrophobia...**
a) a fear of dirty marks
b) a fear of ghosts
c) a fear of looking in mirrors?

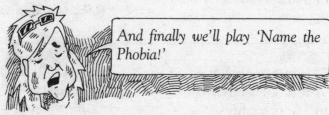

And finally we'll play 'Name the Phobia!'

10 Fear of bees: is it...
a) hivophobia
b) melissophobia
c) buzzaphobia?

11 Fear of horses: is it...
a) hippophobia
b) rhinophobia
c) dobbophobia?

12 Fear of string: is it...
a) ropophobia
b) twineophobia
c) linonophobia?

14 Fear of the number 13: is it...
a) numbophobia
b) unluckyforsomeophobia
c) triskaidekaphobia?

15 Fear of frogs and toads:
is it...
a) taddophobia
b) batrachophobia
c) croakophobia?

How did you get on then? Oh! Just a moment. We've got someone here with another question! It's Mr Stan Duppanfight from Battle in Sussex. What's up Stan?

Excuse me, Stu. But I think you missed out question number 13?

Yes, Stan ... we did! That's because our producer's got triskaidekaphobia ... the fear of the number 13! Oh nuts!

Answers:
1b), 2b), 3a), 4c), 5b), 6c), 7c), 8c), 9c), 10b), 11a), 12c), 14c), 15b)

STORY 6: I WAS A TEENAGE WEREWOLF

Horror story six is a fairly modern one. It's 'I Was A Teenage Werewolf' (1958) by an American called Ralph Thornton. Werewolves have been wandering around the forests of the world for centuries but Ralph decided to put *his* werewolf in an American High School sometime in the 1950s. Of course, the whole tale is totally silly and no such thing would happen in real life but it's still very entertaining. It's got a naughty teenage boy, a pretty girl, a brave cop and a mad scientist. It's the perfect mixture of romance, action and horror that goes to make up the hundreds of stories that are generally known as pulp fiction. In other words stories that keep you amused but don't really cause you to think deep and meaningful thoughts. It's also the sort of story that would make a great horror comic strip. So here it is!

107

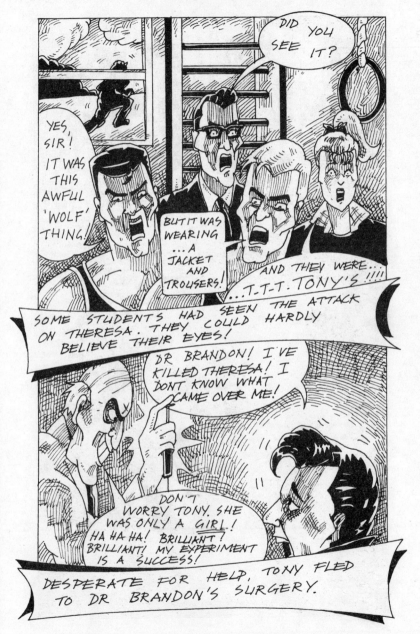

FANTASTIC FACTS 6: THE COMPLETE WEREWOLF – YOUR QUESTIONS ANSWERED

1 WHAT EXACTLY IS A WEREWOLF AND WHERE'S THE BEST PLACE TO FIND ONE?

A werewolf is someone who can turn into a wolf, or wolf-like creature, then back into a person again. The word 'werewolf' comes from two Anglo-Saxon words: *wer*, which means man, and *wulf*, which means wolf.

The forests of France are your best bet for werewolf hunting, but you're probably about four hundred years too late. Between 1520 and 1630, over 30,000 werewolf incidents were reported in France. If you do go looking for French werewolves, remember to ask for *loups-garoux*, as that's what they're called over there.

2 I AM INTERESTED IN BECOMING A WEREWOLF. WHAT ARE THE BEST WAYS TO DO THIS?

Whatever turns you loopy really. Any of the following will do nicely:

a) Find a sheep that's been killed by a wolf, then eat it (the sheep, not the wolf).

b) Find a wolf's footprint. The local safari park's probably best for this. Wait for it to rain. Get down on your hands and knees. Drink the water from the footprint. No cheating ... e.g. filling the print with fizzy pop.

c) Eat a wolf's brains. You'll need to visit a trendy 'delicatessen'-type food shop for these as they're not usually available in ordinary supermarkets.

d) Drink from a stream where wolves have been drinking.

e) Finally, if you're the odd-bod type who's into all manner of weirdness, you can go for the full *magic-ritual-at-midnight* option, which is as follows. Go to the forest. Draw a large circle on the ground. Set a cauldron of magic herbs bubbling in the centre of the circle. Take off all your clothes. Rub fat from a dead cat all over your body. Put on a belt made from wolfskin. Kneel on the ground. Raise your arms over the cauldron. Chant nice things about wolves, e.g. 'Wolves are jolly decent types! Wolves are jolly decent types...' etc.

3 HOW CAN I TELL IF I HAVE BECOME A WEREWOLF?

Look at this diagram. If you have got any of the following there is a chance you have become a werewolf or are becoming one:

SMALL POINTY EARS

BUSHY EYEBROWS THAT MEET IN THE MIDDLE

HAIRY PALMS

THIRD FINGER THE SAME LENGTH AS THE SECOND

LONG CURVED FINGERNAILS

FUR ON THE INSIDE OF YOUR SKIN *

HAIRY FEET

*Some werewolves kept their identity concealed by wearing their fur *under* their skin. Whenever they wanted to go ravaging they would just reverse it (like wearing your fur-lined anorak inside out). Authorities who suspected someone of being a werewolf in the old days would sort of 'peel' them (like a banana) to check for internal fur. (Yes, absolutely disgusting ... but this *is* a *horror* book!)

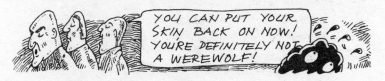

YOU CAN PUT YOUR SKIN BACK ON NOW! YOU'RE DEFINITELY NOT A WEREWOLF!

Generally speaking, if you find yourself getting the urge to behave 'differently' (especially when there's a full moon), e.g. wanting to walk on all fours, howl at the moon, sniff other people's bottoms, that sort of thing – you are probably going a bit 'wolfy'.

4 OK! BUT HOW DO I TURN MYSELF INTO A HUMAN AGAIN?

No problem. Once you've finished your night's werewolfing you should automatically change back into a human as the sun comes up. However, if for some reason or other this doesn't happen, try rolling in the dirt or the morning dew as this will often do the trick.

ME... ROLL AROUND IN THE DIRT?!!... THAT'S WHAT *ANIMALS* DO!

5 IF I MEET A WEREWOLF, HOW CAN I TELL IT IS ONE, AND NOT JUST AN ORDINARY WOLF?

Easy! When someone turns into a werewolf their eyes remain completely human. So what you're looking for is a wolf with human eyes. However, this can be a bit tricky as you have to get up really close to the wolf to check out its peepers, by which time it may well have wolfed you down.

CAN I HAVE A LOOK AT YOUR EYES, NICE GENTLE MR WOLF?!

DUNNO ABOUT THAT, BUT I'LL SHOW YER ME *TEETH!*

6 OUR NEIGHBOURHOOD IS BEING TROUBLED BY A WEREWOLF – WHAT'S THE BEST WAY TO GET RID OF THIS NUISANCE?

Shouldn't be too much trouble if you follow this simple 'Waste A Werewolf' plan:

What you need:
Some silver bullets. They're the only sort that will break the werewolf curse.
To finish the job properly you will need extra weapons such as a pitchfork, an axe, or a knife. Some holy water would be useful, as werewolves are really terrified of this. NB A gun to fire the silver bullets would probably come in handy too.

What to do:
First find the wolf. This is absolutely essential and will greatly increase your chances of killing it. After distracting the furry fiend with a cheery cry of 'Hi, wolfy! Oh look, a *lamb chop*!' blow its brains out. Then give it a few vicious jabs with the pitchfork for good measure, cut off its head with the axe and burn it (the wolf, not the axe). Finally, to break the curse for ever, scatter the wolf's ashes on the ground. To avoid a mouthful of toasted werewolf-flakes, make sure the wind's blowing away from you when you do this.

119

Useful tip: If you later discover that in your hurry to rid your neighbourhood of the hairy menace you have ritually killed and cremated the Alsatian from the local chip shop, avoid bragging about your heroic deed in wayside inns and taverns.

7 I RECENTLY DID A WEREWOLF SURVEY IN MY AREA AND COULDN'T FIND ANY! ACCORDING TO THE BOOKS I'VE READ, IT SEEMS THAT IN THE OLDEN DAYS YOU COULDN'T WALK 50 METRES WITHOUT BUMPING INTO ONE. SO WHERE HAVE THEY ALL GONE?

Good question! Well, at one time, especially in sixteenth-century Europe, there were reports of werewolves all over the place. This was probably due to three things:

a) The forests of Europe were full of perfectly normal and dangerous wolves.

b) The average peasant in the forest had the IQ of an extremely rotten tree stump and less general knowledge than a very small lump of mud, so you could feed them all sorts of superstitious claptrap and codswallop and the pathetic sadwits would believe every word of it.

c) People couldn't get good quality cheap contact lenses and spectacles like they can nowadays.

The apparent lack of werewolves in modern times may also be due to things like efficient electric razors and facial hair removal systems, aromatherapy, family counselling and regular inspections of children by school nurses.

8 IS IT JUST MEN WHO BECOME WEREWOLVES?

No, according to legend, women become werewolves too, as the following scary story will show.

Many years ago a hunter was setting out on an expedition when his nobleman neighbour said to him, 'Bring me something back!' A few hours later, the hunter was attacked by a huge wolf. During his struggle with the beast he managed to cut off one of its paws, which caused it to run off (or maybe just round in circles?). He put the paw in his bag with the rest of his catch.

Meeting the nobleman outside his castle, the hunter reached into his bag for the paw and handed it to him. However, they were both horrified to see that the paw had now turned into a bloody human hand with a gold ring on one of its fingers. The nobleman was even more horrified because he recognized the ring! It belonged to his wife! He took the hand from the hunter and rushed upstairs to his kitchen where he found his wife with her right arm hidden under her apron.

'Show me your right arm!' he cried.

'Why?' said the woman. 'What do you take me for...?'

'A werewolf!' cried the nobleman. 'The game's up, fungus-face!'

And with that he lifted up her apron to find that where her right hand should be there was just a bloody stump!

'Owzat!' he cried. And, ignoring her howls of protest, he dragged her off to the local werewolf exterminator, who immediately burnt her to death to teach her a lesson she'd never forget!

9 WHY DID PEOPLE TRY TO TURN THEMSELVES INTO WEREWOLVES?

Mainly so they could take terrible revenge on their enemies without being recognized. Of course, an easier (and safer) way of getting revenge on someone, would be to spread rumours that *they* were a werewolf, then have the satisfaction of seeing them get shot, peeled or burned at the stake.

10 IS THERE SUCH A THING AS A GOOD WEREWOLF?

Yes, there is. One werewolf is said to have helped a drunken priest who had fallen from his horse and knocked himself out. As darkness descended and the priest lay bleeding on the forest floor, a pack of wild cats smelled his blood and came to finish him off. Just as they were about to sink their claws into him a huge werewolf bounded out of the darkness and scared them off. It then helped the priest to his feet and took him back to his monastery. When morning came the werewolf turned back into an important member of the church who immediately gave the priest a good telling-off for getting so badly sozzled. (Boring ... or what?)

STORY 7: DR JEKYLL AND MR HYDE

Do you have some days when you're a complete angel but others when you're peskier than a piranha in a pilchard pond? Well, if you do, then maybe you've got what is known as a 'Jekyll and Hyde' personality. This way of describing someone who swings wildly between being a goody-two-shoes and an absolute monster, comes from the title of story seven – 'The Strange Case of Dr Jekyll and Mr Hyde' (1886) by Robert Louis Stevenson (1850–1894).

Robert Louis Stevenson

Robert knew that deep down quite a lot of people would like to do naughty things. He also knew that, generally speaking, they don't. That's because most people realize that if we all let the bad side of our personality loose whenever we felt like it, society would quickly collapse into a terrifying and chaotic mess. His great idea for the story, which came to him in a dream, is that good and kind Dr Jekyll discovers a chemical formula that can change him into another person who he decides to call Mr Hyde. As Mr Hyde he can get up to all the wicked stuff he's ever wanted to do without feeling guilty or worrying what other people will think. And he has another formula that will turn him back into Dr Jekyll. Unfortunately his experiment goes very wrong and he starts becoming the evil Mr Hyde ... even when he *doesn't* want to! And *without* using the formula! Perhaps it would do Dr Jekyll good to own up to all his wicked ways in *Shocking True Confessions* magazine?

'My WICKED WICKED Ways'
Dr Henry Jekyll owns up

Dearest reader,
        Before I begin I must make one thing clear. During this confession, I may occasionally become a little ... er ... 'over-excited', even somewhat ... irritable. Please forgive me if this happens. I trust I have made myself clear... OR ARE YOU TOO STUPID TO UNDERSTAND THE SIMPLEST OF IDEAS, YOU BRAIN-DEAD BLOWFLY! YOU MAGGOT-MINDED

Me

LITTLE "BOOKWORM"! YOU PATHETIC OBJECT THAT'S JUST SLITHERED OUT OF THE STEAMING BOTTOM OF A FRESHLY DEAD PLAGUE RAT... Oh oh, it's begun already! Forgive me. Just a moment I must refresh myself with a draught from my flask. Please... please... be patient. SLURP, GULP, SLURP. Ah! That's better. That should see me OK (for a while at least). I do apologize for that outburst. Now I will begin my story:

I was born in the year 19 and something or other. After growing up in a rich family I decided I would become a medical researcher as I wished to help relieve suffering and help my fellow human beings. I was successful in my career and soon gained the respect of all around me. In my spare time I enjoyed myself in ways which some people might consider rather, er...'naughty', so I will not go into them here. Naturally, I kept this side of my life private. I worked hard in my profession and the world saw me as a good and decent man. But all the time I knew that (just like ALL human beings) I had TWO sides to my character. The good. And the ... BAD! And I often felt them painfully pulling in opposite directions (reader, maybe YOU have felt this too?). 'Oh!' I thought. 'If only the good part of me could live separately from the bad. Then they could each go their own sweet way and not be forever clashing so inconveniently!'

One day I happened to be noodling around in my laboratory – mixing a little of this with a little of that, making jottings in my notebook and so on – when I chanced upon a formula that would perhaps provide the means for me to bring this very situation about! I wasted no time and mixed a large draught of the potion. I watched it steam and bubble for some seconds, then drank it down. Oh, reader. The AGONY I suffered! My body was gripped by pain! I felt as though my bones were being gnawed by monstrous wolves and my flesh was being mangled by threshing machines. And then, when I thought I could take no more, the pain suddenly disappeared. A feeling of purest pleasure swept over me! I felt as free as a bird. I felt good!

... YEAH, REAL GOOOOOOD, BABY!... The cares that go with constantly having to be decent and respectable were suddenly gone! To be honest... I felt sort of well, er... wicked! YEAH... WELL WICKED - HA HA HA!... The next thing I did was to look in a mirror. I did not recognize myself! I was no longer ME! BABY! I WAS OUTTA SIGHT! HA HA!... The face that stared back at me was warped and twisted by purest evil. My body was shorter by several centimetres, my eyes glittered cunningly and hair had sprouted in places you wouldn't believe. (Please Don't ask!) And my breath! Next to me, the stinkiest sewer would have smelt like roses! Yes! I had become ANOTHER person! An utterly ugly and repulsive creature. But did I care? Of course I didn't! Because now, I could be... BAAAAD! OOH YEAH! SOOOO BAAAAAAD. OOH! OOH! OOH! WAS I EXCITED! YEH! YEH! HEH HEH HEH... Excuse me, another drink, I think. SLURP SLURP.

I decided to call my new, other self, Mr Edward Hyde. Now came the difficult bit. Could I turn back to the OLD me? I checked the jottings

of my formula, mixed the second
potion and drank it down. Again
I was racked by terrible pain but it
quickly passed and once more I became
my old self — good kind, caring Dr Henry
Jekyll! 'Brilliant!' I thought. 'What a
discovery! I can turn myself from
one person to the other whenever I
wish. I can lead the PERFECT double
life! In the shape of Mr Edward Hyde
I can be evil, naughty and wicked to
my heart's content and not be
bothered in the least by the conscience
of that old fuss-pot and do-gooder, Dr
'Dull Trousers' Jekyll.'

I bought a suit of clothes for
Mr Hyde and rented him a
house in Soho from which
he / I / we could get up to all
manner of jiggery-pokery. Ooh ooh!
Boy were we / he / I going to have fun!
Just so that my (extremely dim-
witted) servants wouldn't
be alarmed if they saw
me returning from my
evil outings still in my
HYDE-OUS state... HA HA!... I told
them that a certain Mr Edward
Hyde would occasionally be visiting

my house and they were to treat him as my special guest. clever... or what?

So then I began my double life. I got up to all manner of delicious wickedness in the shape of Mr Hyde. I will not describe it here... AND IT'S NONE OF YOUR BUSINESS...SO BOG OFF, STICKY BEAK! Sorry, sorry! Hang on... SLURP SLURP... Then, to resume my Jekyll identity, I would just swig potion number two. The very potion (as you will have no doubt guessed by now) that I am having to sip more and more as I write this confession!

On returning from my wild adventures I felt no shame or sorrow. Back in the shape of 'goody-goody' Dr Jekyll, I said to myself, 'Do not fret! It was not YOU that did those terrible things. It was that awful Mr Hyde!' And my conscience would be clear! HA!

Things went on like this for some time, with me thoroughly enjoying my two lives of evil-good-for-nothing and fine-upstanding-citizen. Then a little problem occurred

One day I was returning to my house in the shape of Mr Hyde when I bumped into a small girl and knocked her over. She was a sweet little thing and, like me, she hadn't been looking where she was going ... BUT SHE SHOULD HAVE BEEN, SHOULDN'T SHE! THE STUPID, SNOTTY NOSED, LITTLE ANKLE - BITER! SO IT SERVED HER RIGHT, DIDN'T IT, WHEN I TRAMPLED ALL OVER HER IN MY HOB - NAILED BOOTS! HA HA HA! OOOH OOOH HMMMM... THE MEMORY OF HER TERRIFIED SHRIEKS STILL FILLS ME WITH DEEPEST PLEASURE, OOH OOH...

Oh dear! Do excuse me. More potion! A TRIPLE dose this time, I think! SLURP SLURP SLURP. After the accident I was immediately surrounded by passers-by and the girl's parents who had all seen my terrible cruelty. But fortunately, I was able to buy them off with a cheque. It was a narrow escape!

After this, my double life continued reasonably smoothly, though I suspect that my two best friends, Mr Utterson and Dr Lanyon, were becoming more and more concerned about my friendship with the evil Edward Hyde. Not only had they heard that he was visiting my house, but Utterson had actually seen the terrible accident with the little girl!

Then one morning, something odd happened. As I awoke and stretched to switch on my bedside radio I noticed that the hand that reached for the 'ON' button was all twisted and covered with spiky hair.

'Funny!' I thought to myself. 'I'm sure I went to bed as Dr Jekyll!' I pulled back the bed covers for a swift shufty at my body. Reader! I was now MR HYDE! I had changed overnight! But I had NOT taken the potion. I was panic-stricken! I lay trembling for some time, thinking what this could mean. Then I made a decision. 'Enough is enough!' I thought. 'It is a pity, but it MUST be done! I am meddling with something that has slipped from my control. I will use the potion to return myself to my Dr Jekyll state and then, from this day on, I will cease my wicked double life for EVER!'

I did as I had vowed and for weeks I remained entirely Dr Jekyll. I did many good works and did not think one single bad or shameful thought. But reader, you know how it is, don't you? As time passes, the effects of a shock wear off. With the ordinariness of everyday life, boredom sets in, doesn't it? So after two whole months of perfect goodness, I thought to myself, 'Oh what the heck! Why not! They say a 'change' is as good as a rest, don't they!' ... HA HA HA! ... So without any more hesitation I swigged down a shot of potion OOH! OOH! SLURP, SLURP. Moments later, back in my old 'Hyde-bound' state, I scampered out into the night, feeling absolutely brilliant, and eager to be up to mischief! I hadn't gone far when I was approached by an elderly, silver-haired gentleman. He appeared to be lost. He did nothing more than ever-so-politely ask me for directions. But as he did, something inside me <u>SNAPPED!</u> ... THE OLD DUFFER REALLY GOT UP MY NOSE. I HURLED MYSELF AT HIM AND STRUCK HIM AGAIN AND AGAIN

WITH MY HEAVY WALKING STICK AS I RAINED A THOUSAND BLOWS ON HIS FRAIL OLD BODY AND LISTENED TO THE SICKENING SOUND OF HIS FRAGILE BONES SHATTERING AND HIS PATHETIC SCREAMS FOR MERCY, I THOUGHT, 'OH YES. THIS IS...FUN!' AFTER A FEW MORE MINUTES OF BELTING THE OLD TWIT SENSELESS, I RAN OFF, CHUCKLING GLEEFULLY AND QUIVERING ALL OVER WITH PLEASURE.

SLURP, SLURP. The next morning, back in my Dr Jekyll identity, I turned on the breakfast news and got two terrible shocks! Not only had the old chap died from his injuries but my crime had been recorded by CCTV cameras in the street where I'd attacked him. I, or rather, Hyde, was now a wanted man! A MURDERER no less! And of course, Hyde was known. He'd got a house and a bank account. So that was that! I could no longer enjoy my wicked adventures in the shape of Mr Edward Hyde. I had to remain Dr Jekyll to save my skin. But fortunately, unlike other

criminals, I had no need to lie low.
Well I was the upstanding, respectable
and good doctor, wasn't I? Feeling
thankful for my escape, I decided
that this was the end of Hyde for <u>ALL</u>
time. After his terrible crime I would
spend the rest of my life doing good
works and kind deeds to make up for
his wickedness. And of course, I would
still be able to go out and enjoy all
my old <u>RESPECTABLE</u> pleasures,
like walking the streets of
London and observing the
comings and goings of my
fellow humans.

During one of these trips, a few
days later, I was sitting on a bench
in Regent's Park. I was enjoying the
spring birdsong and the sight of
happy people all around me when I
happened to glance down. What a shock
I got! My clothes were <u>GROWING</u> on
me! My hands were fast
disappearing into the arms of my
jacket and my shoes had become
almost entirely hidden by
my ever lengthening trousers! And
then the awful truth struck me! My
clothes <u>WEREN'T</u> growing. It was me

that was shrinking! I was turning into Hyde again. Without the potion! And for all the world to see! For a moment I was paralysed with terror. Hyde's picture had been in all the newspapers. I would be spotted and arrested! Pulling my coat over my face, I hurried from the park and hailed a taxi. I told the driver to take me to a hotel. As soon as I got there I hired a room and hid away until I could think what to do next. The potion that I needed to become Dr Jekyll again was in the laboratory at my house. I couldn't go there as I was now entirely Hyde, the wanted murderer! I did have SOMETHING of Jekyll's though — I could still produce my old handwriting. I quickly scrawled a note to my old friend Dr Lanyon, asking him to go to my laboratory and get me a certain flask marked X. I then handed the note to the hotel messenger boy, taking care to hide my face.

Later that evening, under cover of darkness, I made my way to Lanyon's house where I knew he would now have the potion. I cannot go into the details of our meeting. It is too painful for me to recall. All I will say is that my dear friend saw my transformation from Hyde to Jekyll take place. Reader, the shock was too much for him to bear. Within a few weeks my old friend was dead of a heart attack!

Some weeks have passed since these events. To avoid the prying eyes of my neighbours and servants I have locked myself in my laboratory. I am taking larger and larger doses of the potion but they no longer seem to be having the desired effect. The evil power of Edward Hyde is getting stronger and stronger. I have downed vast quantities of the potion in order to write this confession in my Jekyll state. Nevertheless I fear that the beast within me is now taking over completely ... WHAT DO I MEAN FEAR? I WELCOME IT! WHY WOULD I WANT TO BE THAT PATHETIC LILY-LIVERED, NAMBY-PAMBY, MILKSOP, JEKYLL! I HATE HIM WITH ALL MY BEING AND WOULD DESTROY HIM WITH THE GREATEST OF PLEASURE — — AS I WOULD ANYONE WHO MIGHT TRY TO DEPRIVE ME OF MY WICKED INDULGENCES! AND THAT INCLUDES YOU! YOU NOSY LITTLE TOAD OF A READER!

YOU SUCKER OF SCUM, YOU BATHER IN WARM PIGSWILL, YOU SNIFFER OF TOILET SEATS! GET YOUR FILTHY LITTLE NOSE OUT OF MY BUSINESS OR I'LL... I'LL...! NOW WHAT IS THAT? THERE'S A BANGING ON THE LABORATORY DOOR! IT'S THAT INTERFERING FOOL UTTERSON AGAIN! HE SPOTTED ME AT THE WINDOW AND HE'S YELLING, 'WE KNOW YOU'RE IN THERE HYDE! WHAT HAVE YOU DONE WITH DR JEKYLL? IF YOU HAVE MURDERED HIM IT WILL BE THE WORSE FOR YOU. OPEN THIS DOOR AT ONCE OR I WILL BREAK IT DOWN!' HEH HEH HEH! JUST LET HIM TRY. WHAT I DID TO THE OLD MAN WILL BE NOTHING COMPARED TO WHAT I'LL DO TO UTTERSON... Oh oh! WHAT am I saying? SLURP. SLURP. Utterson is my oldest and dearest friend. We have known each other since we were boys. I think I can endure this torture no longer. If I am to save the life of my dearest friend I have to sacrifice my own. There is only one path open to me now...

FOOTNOTE:

This true confession was found by Mr Utterson after he had broken down the door of Dr Jekyll's laboratory. Next to it lay the body of Mr Edward Hyde.

Owen Up, Editor, Shocking True Confessions Magazine

FANTASTIC FACTS 7: DIPPY DOCTORS AND BATTY BOFFINS

Horror stories are just bursting with potty profs and quazy quacks like Henry Jekyll. It's obvious why! If you want something utterly horrendous and incredible to happen in your horror story, like having someone sprout enormous red whiskers all over their eyeballs, or grow as big as a shopping mall ... screwy scientists and mad medics are just the people to have around. They can make just about *anything* happen and are the modern version of the magicians and sorcerers that used to cause so much mischief in fairy tales. These cranky kinds are definitely the sorts who have their own websites, so let's surf the net and meet some of them.

1 Dr Xavier
Hi! I'm the mad doctor in the film *The Man with the X-Ray Eyes* (1963).
My discovery: I invent a special solution that enables me to see right through things ... including *clothes*.
(Yes, I thought that would make you *blush*!)
My story: I get a bit nutty about my research, especially when my bosses won't give me any extra dosh for it. My pal tries to calm me down so I kill him, then go on the run and work at a carnival as Mentalo, "the man who sees all". And I do see *all* you know (so come out of that cupboard, now!).

2 Dr Raymond

I'm the mental medic in the *The Great God Pan* (1894) by A Machen.

My potty project: I perform brain surgery on a woman called Mary because I want her to 'make contact' with other worlds and beings.

My story: Unfortunately, I make a right botch of the job and end up completely destroying Mary's mind. (Well, no one's perfect, you know). Later on Mary gives birth to a baby girl. And this is where it gets really interesting. The girl grows up to be very weird. All of her boyfriends have a tendency to die or commit suicide. Eventually she also pops her clogs and afterwards sort of 'melts' and changes from a woman to a man ... then to a beast ... and then to something even worse than a beast. (No, not a TV show host ... my story isn't that horrendous!)

3 Dr Phibes

Greetings, victims! I'm the gibbering GP in the film *The Abominable Dr Phibes* (1971).

My story: I have a car crash in which my wife is killed and I lose my face. (You know, I still haven't found it ... ha ha!) I feel very angry with the surgeons who operated on my wife after the accident and blame them for not saving her life.

My project: I take my revenge on the surgeons by destroying them with plagues like the ones the Egyptians got zapped with in the Bible: loads of locusts, flotillas of frogs and regiments of rats – that sort of thing. Is this mad enough for you?

4 Dr Moreau

That's not mad ... I'm mad! Welcome to my island in the Pacific. I'm the brilliant but completely potty prof in *The Island Of Dr Moreau* (1896) by H G Wells.

My project: I've got a laboratory where I chop up animals like bears and bulls and pigs, then stitch 'em back together as half-beast, half-humans. Don't look so shocked ... it's tons of fun! (And it sure beats writing out prescriptions for cough medicine.)

5 Dr Gogol

I'm the quazy quack in the movie *Mad Love* (1935). And I'm a real fruitcake!

My story: I'm in love with Yvonne. But she doesn't love me! Then her concert-pianist husband injures his hands so badly that they have to be amputated.

My project: I give hubby some nice new hands which I get from the guillotined body of a knife-throwing murderer! Then I convince hubby that his new hands have thrown a knife which has killed his own father (but it was me really ... tee hee!). My plan is to drive hubby nutty so I can have Yvonne for myself. Just to make sure he really does flip his lid I also pretend to be the guillotined murderer, complete with new steel hands and head sewn back on! Ha ha ha! Told you I was bonkers!

6 Dr Caligari

If you zink zose lot are mad you should get a load of zis! My project: I heff got my own pet murderer zat I keep in a big box. Zat is why my film is called *The Cabinet of Dr Caligari* (1919). It was the first big horror movie success ever. And talk about veird!

My story: Zere are so many tvists and turns in ze plot of my film zat I zink zat you too vill also be batty ven you heff finished vatching it!

7 Professor Quatermass

Hi! I'm Bernard Quatermass and you'll be relieved to know that I'm not a bit barmy. The only weird thing about me is my name. However, I do like to go around sticking my nose into scary situations.

My story: My favourite and most horrific adventure, *Quatermass and the Pit*, took place when some workmen digging the foundations for an office block found a five-million-year-old space-ship containing mummified aliens. Me and some other brainy sorts investigated and the more we snooped the more terrified we got. We found out that the hobgoblins and demons that everyone else thought were just old folk legends really had existed. They were the aliens who'd landed on earth millions of years ago and sort of 'mixed' with normal people. And when me and my pals disturbed them, the results were really horrifying! After watching this spooky series on TV in 1959, lots of British kids went to bed scared out of their jim-jams!

8 Dr Griffin

Hello. I am here you know. It's just that you can't see me. I'm the daffy doc who invents a drug that sends me invisible in the novel *The Invisible Man* (1897) by H G Wells and again in the film of the book.

My story: Unfortunately, my invisibility drug has the rather inconvenient side effect of sending me as screwy as a soap sud! So I get up to all sorts of naughtiness like murder and robbery and soon the police are after me. Also, to become invisible I have to take off all my clothes. 'So what?' I hear you say. Well, have you tried running around completely nude, in 15 centimetres of snow, with a load of cops chasing you? Chattering teeth and completely non-invisible footprints have a tendency to give the game away, you know!

9 Dr Cyclops

Hey, stupid surfers, get a load of me! I've also got my own *Dr Cyclops* film (1940) and my planet-saving project is BRILLIANT!

My project: I am an environmentalist! So what do you think I am going to do to save the world's resources? It's simple, you dummy! I am going to shrink everyone in the world to just one tenth of their normal size. That way they will use up hardly anything. (Just think how much toilet paper we would save if we all had bums the size of plums.)

My story: Everything was going brilliantly down at my laboratory in the Peruvian rain forest ... apart from one thing! These pesky eyes of mine are so bad that I can't see down my microscope. So I get some other scientists to help me. Then I shrink them! But then the ungrateful little creatures deliberately break my specs! It's the beginning of the end for me!

10 Dr Marvin

Yo! I'm the idiotic inventor in the horror film *Screamers* (1982).

My project: I have created a race of mutant amphibians in my laboratory and also learned to communicate with the really dangerous sea-apes who live in the lost city of Atlantis. (Surely you know about them!)

My story: My boss is trying to get the treasure of the lost city of Atlantis from the bottom of the lagoon on the island he owns but it's far too deep for humans to explore. He plans to use my mutant amphibians and my talkative sea-apes to do this (the cheeky blighter!). When he has got the goodies he is also planning to run off with my beautiful daughter too (some people!). But he hasn't reckoned on Dr Claude (yes, another doctor ... they're everywhere aren't they!) who also fancies my daughter. It's all very perplexing and ever so horrific! I ask you ... who'd be a mad scientist?

So who do you think was screwiest then? Perhaps you'd better not make up your mind until you've read story eight in which you're going to meet the most famous horror-story scientist of all time...

STORY 8: FRANKENSTEIN

Horror story number eight is the hyper-mega-famous, 'Frankenstein' (1818) by Mary Shelley (1797–1851). It's the story of a student called Victor Frankenstein who thinks he's doing the world a big favour when he sets about creating a living human being from odd body bits which he picks up in graveyards and operating theatres. But he's wrong! Almost as soon as he's finished the job he starts to hate the creature he's made and wishes never to see it again. But where does this leave his eight-foot-tall creation? It doesn't know where it's come from, people it meets in the street are terrified of it and most of all ... it wants a friend! It regrets the day it was made and starts to hate whoever put it together in the first place. Victor and his creature are both deeply troubled and unhappy. Their mounting personal problems become more horrific as each day passes. If they were around today they'd probably have been seeking advice from an agony aunt right from the outset of this terrible tale.

Ask Agatha

*Your most painful and personal
questions answered.
Strictest secrecy guaranteed —
WHATEVER the problem!*

Dear Agatha,

I've got a few questions you may be able to help me with. Since beginning my university course I've been very keen to make a big scientific discovery which will help the human race in some way. Well, after working my socks off for ages, I've come up with an amazing find! I've discovered the secret of giving life to dead flesh! With the right ingredients and lots of hard graft(s), I am sure that I can now actually create a living human being! WOW! So my questions are: 1) Do you think it's OK for me to go ahead with this project? 2) Will it be of benefit to mankind? 3) Have you any ideas where I might pick up the necessary bits and pieces, e.g. legs, a good-quality belly-button, ears, kidneys, eyelashes, veins, etc., etc.?

Victor

Dear Victor,

Nice one. And yes, go for it, kid! Sounds like you're on to a real winner. If you can pull this one off, the world will thank you for it. Now, regarding the odds and ends you'll need. No probs! Just sneak into the university dissecting laboratory or pop down the local graveyard when no one's about! There's usually lots of that sort of stuff just 'lying around' in those places. Ha ha. And it won't cost you an 'arm and a leg'! Ha ha ha. But make sure you don't get caught 'red-handed'! Ha ha ha ha. Let me know how you get on.
Best of luck,

Agatha

Dear Agatha,

Sorry to have taken so long in getting back to you. My 'creation' has taken up all of my time. For the last 2 years I have been up to ~~my~~ ...
sorry ... its neck in it! But now I have stuck on its head! So 'he' is just about done and will be strutting his stuff any day. Will keep you posted.

Victor

Dear Victor,

Don't worry about how long it's taking! Anything worth doing is worth doing well! That's what I always say! And I'm sure your great project will turn out to be a monster success! Can't wait to hear how you get on!
Cheers,

Agatha

Dear Agatha,

Oh no! Oh no! Oh no! What have I gone and done? Yesterday was going to be the BIG day. The climax of all my hard work! There was my creation (all eight feet of him) stretched out on the table. I threw the switches and zapped the power into him. He shuddered, he twitched, he jerked (boy, did he jerk!) then, bit by bit, he rose from the table. And finally he ... grinned at me! Agatha, I flipped! Those watery eyes of his just freaked me out. They were gross!

I took off out of there like a scientist with a wasp up his test-tube. Luckily, I hadn't been out long when I bumped into my best pal, Henry Clerval. We went for a drink and were soon chatting and laughing like we hadn't a care in the world. In no time at all I'd forgotten the terrible events of just a few hours  *earlier. Even better! When I got home again the creature had vanished. 'Hoorah!' I thought. 'Good riddance. I never want to see the filthy monster again!'*

I'm feeling better now that I've got all this off my chest. And I suppose it could have all turned out much worse. I'm telling you Ag, that's the last time I go messing with nature! Phew, what a narrow escape that was.
All the best,

Victor

Dear Victor,

Don't take on so, love. No one's perfect. And don't forget! We all learn by our mistakes. You may find this hard to believe, but even I sometimes make them! (Hardly ever though!) Anyway, you're probably best rid of the thing. Sounds absolutely hideous to me! Definitely not the sort of creature I'd want anything to do with!
All the best,

Agatha

DEAR AGAFFA

I HAVE NOT EVER WRITTEN TO YOU BEFORE BUT I WAS WONDERING IF YOU COULD HELPING ME? HERE IS MY PROBLEM. AGAFFA, YOU KNOW HOW MOST PEOPLES HAVE MUMMIES AND DADDIES AND WHATNOTS? WELL, I DO NOT GOT ANY AT ALL AND IT IS UPSETTING ME NO END! ALSO NO MATTER HOW MUCH I AM RACKETING MY BRAINS I DO NOT EVER REMEMBER BEING A BOY-BABY OR A TWEENAGER. MY FIRST EVER MEMORY IS WAKING UP ON A TABLE ALL FULLY GROWED UP. A YOUNG CHAP WAS LOOKING AT ME BUT NEXT MINUTE HE RUNNED AWAY! I DO NOT THINK HE LIKE ME MUCH. I THOUGHT 'NO SENSE IN LYING HERE. I'LL CHECK OUT THE NEIGHBOURHOOD!' SO I PUT ON A BIG COAT AND WENT IN STREETS. BUT PEOPLE CRIED WORDINGS LIKE 'UUURGH LOOKS AT THAT! WHAT A FREAK-BOD.

WHAT A UGLY-MUG THAT IS... IF EVER I SAW ONE!' THEN ALL THEY RANNED AWAY AND SHOUTED 'LOOK OUT EVERYONE. A MONSTER IS COMING!' SO MAYBE THAT IS WHO I AM? PLEASE HELP ME. I AM SAD AS A POTATO.

YOURS TEARFULLY

A. MONSTER

Dear A. Monster,

Don't worry, luvvie. You're suffering from what we call an 'identity' crisis. It will pass. And take no notice of the cruel things that people say to you in the street. They're probably jealous. I bet you're really quite a handsome hunk! And I'm sure your memory loss is only temporary. Maybe you were dropped on your head when you were a baby? Try to get out more and make new friends. If you don't mind me saying so, I think your English would benefit from some extra work. Have you thought of attending GCSE evening classes?
Keep your chin up,

Agatha

DEAR A GAFFA
I HAVE WENTED OUT LIKE YOU SAID AND FOUND A FAMILY TO BE FRIENDS WITH. I DO NOT WANT THEM TO SEE ME BECAUSE I AM WORRIED THEY MIGHT RUN AWAY LIKE ALL THE OTHERS DID. I AM HIDING IN THEIR SHED AND WATCHING ALL THEIR COMINGS AND GOINGS (TEE HEE!) AT NIGHT I COME OUT AND DO THEIR WOOD CHOPPING AND STUFF. BUT THEY DO NOT KNOW IT'S ME! (TEE HEE HEE!) THEY ARE ALL NICE AND I DO LOVE THEM ALL LOTS AND LOTS AND LOTS. I THINK THAT SOON I WILL SOON SHOW MYSELF TO THEM. THEN WE WILL BE FRIENDS AND LIVE

IN BIG HAPPY FAMILY LIKE I NEVER HAD BEFORE!

. A. MONSTER

P.S. I HAVE FINDED SOME PAPERS IN THE POCKET OF MY BIG COAT. THEY ARE WRITINGS BY SOMEONE CALLED FRANKENSTEIN. ALL JOTTINGS AND SCRIBBLES ABOUT BUILDING A CREATURE. SO I THINK THAT IS PROBABLY WHERE I HAVE CAME FROM! WELL... BLOW ME DOWN!

Dear A. Monster,

That's the ticket, luvvie! I just know you're going to bond with your new family when you finally meet up. And listen, handsome, they'll probably be so delighted when they finally see you that they'll go absolutely bananas! About those papers you found in your pocket – forget them, dear!

This Frankenstein's probably some saddo crank who's got nothing better to do with his time. What really matters is you and how you feel about yourself!

Love and kisses,

Agatha

DEAR AGAFFA

BOO HOO HOOO HOOO. NOW I AM SAD AS TWO THOUSAND POTATOES! YESTERDAY I SHOWED MYSELF TO MY LOVELY FAMILY AND THEY ALL SAID I WAS BIG UGLY MONSTER DEMON THING AND RAN AWAY! JUST LIKE ALL THE OTHER ONES BEFORE... BUT WORSE CAME THEN. THE MEN CAME BACK WITH DOGS AND GUNS TO KILL ME. OH BOO HOO HOO HOO... I AM BIG UGLY SCHMUK AND NO ONE LOVES ME IN WHOLE WIDE WORLD. WHY DID THAT NASTY FRANKENSTEIN MAN MAKE ME? JUST FOR ME TO BE UNHAPPY, I THINK. I HATE HIM TO PIECES BOO HOO HOO.

A MONSTER

Dear A. Monster,

Oh dear. I am sorry to hear about your failure to hit it off with your new chums. It seems to me that you need to do some work on your inter-personal skills, luvvie. Some of us are just born with the natural ability to relate to others and some aren't. And it looks like you have the social skills of a rabid rodent! This Frankenstein chap – whoever he is! – has certainly got a lot to answer for. What a rotter!

Yours,

Agatha

Dear Agatha,

I am sorry to have to write to you again but it seems to be one thing after another just lately! First off, I have been very ill for some time. I think it may be the result of two years non-stop work on the creature followed by the shock of his final appearance. Then, just when I was beginning to feel a bit better, I got terrible news from home. My little brother has been murdered! And to make matters worse, our maid, who we all loved, has been found guilty of his murder and executed. The family are devastated. I have returned

155

home and am doing my best to comfort them. But *Agatha, it is all doing my head in! What do you suggest?*

Victor

Dear Victor,

I am sorry to hear of your sad news. Listen! If you start getting down in the dumps you're going to fall ill again. So you need to keep active. Get your hiking togs on and go for a bracing walk in the mountains. Will you do that for me, luvvie? Believe me, it'll do you the world of good!

Agatha

DEAR AGAFFA
I HAVE GOT SOMETHING TO TELL
YOU THAT I THINK WILL MAKE YOU VERY,
VERY ANGRY WITH ME. I HAVE BEEN VERY,
VERY NAUGHTY! AFTER THOSE PEOPLE WITH
THE GUNS CHASED ME AWAY I WALKED
ROUND FEELING VERY SAD AND ANGRY.
THEN I MET A LITTLE BOY AND
THOUGHT THAT MAYBE <u>HE WOULD</u>

LIKE TO BE MY FRIEND. SO I SAID 'HELLO THERE, LITTLE CHAP! YOU ARE NICE. WILL YOU BE MY CHUM?' AND HE SAID 'YOU MUST BE JOKING, YOU GREAT BIG UGLY MONSTER, YOU! I THINK YOU WANT TO EAT ME. GO AWAY OR I WILL TELL MY DADDY. HE IS MR FRANKENSTEIN AND HE IS MAYOR OF THIS TOWN. SO BEAT IT, UGLY MUSH!' A GAFFA, THIS MADE ME VERY ANGRY INDEED, ESPECIALLY WHEN I HEARD <u>THAT</u> NAME, THE SAME AS HIM WHAT MADE ME. SO I PICKED UP THE BOY AND GAVE HIM A REAL GOOD SHAKING. BUT THEN HE WENT <u>DEAD</u>. OOER! I DO NOT THINK I KNOW MY OWN STRENGTH.

A. MONSTER

Dear A. Monster,

Well! I was ... erm ... sorry to hear of the unfortunate 'accident' with the little boy. I think the least said about this the better. As you know, I am sworn to keep all confessions a secret. So, if you keep your mouth shut too, I think it'll be OK! Now, to get back to your other problems, I have been thinking about them a lot and have decided that what you really need is a girlfriend! If the opportunity occurs for you to get one, go for it! You will not regret it.

Agatha

Dear Agatha,

Oh no! Oh no! Can things get any worse? I think not! Yesterday, I did as you told me and went for a walk in the mountains. I was sitting on a rock having a breather when I saw a figure approaching from the valley. As it got near I noticed that it was very tall. At least eight feet tall! Yes! It was IT! The creature I had so foolishly created! Before I had a chance to escape, the horrible thing sort of trapped me against the rock face and then

 began telling me its troubles. It went on and on and on you know, moaning about its awful life and its personal problem. (I HATE whingers, don't you?) It blamed ME for all its troubles because it was me who made it in the first place! Would you believe it?! The ungrateful monster! Then it gave me the really shocking news, Agatha! It was it that had killed my dear little brother! As a sort of revenge against

me and my family. 'Oh no!' I thought. 'Am I to be tormented by my monstrous creation for ever more?'

And then it said something that made me think that I can rid myself of this nightmare for ever. It said it would leave me alone if I gave it just one thing. Guess what! It only asked me to make it ... a girlfriend! I mean, the monstrous cheek of it! I said, 'Yes!' (I'd do anything to be rid of this demon!) But what do you think, Agatha? Am I doing the right thing?

Victor

Dear Victor,

Of course you are, luvvie. Don't hesitate, don't wait! Knock it up a mate ... before it's too late, mate! Ha ha.
Love,

Agatha

PS This creature thingy of yours is beginning to remind me of someone. But for the life of me I can't think who. I'm just so busy and I've got a memory like a sieve you know!

DEAR AGAFFA,

THE OTHER DAY I WAS UP A MOUNTAIN AND I BUMPED INTO HIM WHAT MADE ME. WHILE WE WAS HAVING A CHAT I SUDDENLY HAD A GREAT IDEA. I THOUGHT IF HE WOULD MAKE ME MY VERY OWN GIRLFRIEND I WOULD BE AS HAPPY AS A LARRIKIN AND WOULD NOT HAVE TO GO ROUND FRIGHTENING PEOPLE BY TRYING TO BE THEIR FRIEND. HE SAID HE WOULD SO I AM AS CHUFFED AND EXCITED AS CAN BE. I CAN'T WAIT TO MEET HER! I WONDER WHAT COLOUR HER EYES WILL BE?

A. MONSTER

P.S. WHAT IS SNOGGING?

Dear A. Monster,

I'm very excited for you, luvvie! I think this young lady will be the making of you both! OK! Now to snogging. It's something that people do to show they like each other. If you want to know more, send me a cheque for £5.99 and I'll mail you my international bestsellers, First Steps To Snogging and Advanced Snogging For The More Confident Kisser.

Love and lots of kisses,

Agatha

Dear Agatha,

Slightly better news. Me and my pal Clerval are on our hols in Scotland. It's nice and quiet up here so I am taking the opportunity to get on with building the mate for you-know-who! With a bit of luck it will fall head over heels in love with her, then leave me alone for good. Can't wait!
All the best,

Victor

PS Some other good news. I think there is a chance I will be marrying my childhood sweetheart quite soon. So perhaps all is not gloom and doom after all! I'll keep my fingers crossed.

Dear Victor,

I'm so glad to hear that you're getting some 'quality time'! There's nothing like a little hol to recharge the batteries, is there? And talking of charging up batteries ... good luck with the project!

Agatha

PS Your letters are still ringing bells with me but for the life of me I can't think what they're reminding me of! Ah well, not to worry. It looks like everything's going to turn out for the best after all! It really does make me feel good deep down inside to know that I'm able to be of so much help and bring about so many happy endings. It sort of makes the job so ... worthwhile!

DEAR AGAFFA,

THE OTHER DAY I SNEAKED TO THE WINDOW OF THE HUT WHERE FRANKEN-STEIN WAS BUSY BUILDING MY NEW GIRL-FRIEND SO I COULD TAKE A LITTLE PEEP AT HOW SHE WAS COMING ALONG. THERE SHE WAS ON THE TABLE — STILL NOT FINISHED AND WITH A FEW BITS MISSING — BUT STILL LOOKING LOVELY AS ANYTHING. 'LOR, WHAT A CRACKER!' I THOUGHT, AS I GAZED

AT HER. 'A SCRUMMY GIRLFRIEND, ALL OF MY VERY OWN. SHE IS REALLY BEAUTIFUL! AND WHEN HE HAS STUCK ON HER EYES 👁👁 AND HER HAIR 🌀 AND HER TEETH 🦷 AND HER SKIN... SHE WILL BE EVEN MORE BEAUTIFUL!' JUST AT THAT MOMENT FRANKENSTEIN SAW ME PEEPING. FOR SOME REASON IT SEEMED TO GET RIGHT UP HIS NOSE. QUICK AS A FLASH HE PICKED UP MY HALF-BUILT NEW GIRLFRIEND AND THREW HER ACROSS THE ROOM, "SPLAT!" SHE BANGED INTO THE WALL THEN FELL IN A HORRIBLE, MESSY HEAP ON THE FLOOR "SQUELCH" "DRIBBLE, DRIBBLE" "SQUELCH", "FALOLLOP FALOLLOP" AGAFFA! ALL OF A SUDDEN MY NEW GIRLFRIEND WAS BLOODY CAT'S MEAT! AND I HADN'T EVEN SNOGGED HER! (WHATEVER THAT IS.) OH AGAFFA! BOO HOO! BOO HOO! BOO HOO! SNIFFLE... SNIFFLE... SNIFFLE... LIFE IS SO CRUEL! I

HAVE NOW HAD IT UP TO HERE WITH THIS FRANKENSTEIN. HE IS GOING TO GET WHAT'S COMING TO HIM. I HAVE HEARD THAT HE IS GETTING MARRIED TO <u>HIS</u> GIRLFRIEND WELL, WE'LL SEE ABOUT THAT! AND THAT'S NOT ALL. I HAVE GOT ANOTHER NASTY SURPRISE IN STORE FOR HIM. I HAVE REALLY FLIPPED NOW. THERE WILL BE NO STOPPING ME!

A. MONSTER

Dear A. Monster,

Oops! You do get yourself into some pickles, don't you? Now, I hope you don't go and do anything silly, like before? Have you thought of attending anger-management classes? I believe they're very good. Failing that I suggest that you go somewhere quiet and punch a pillow.

Keep cool, luvvie,

Agatha

Dear Agatha,

 Oh no! Oh no! Oh no! My best friend, Clerval, is dead! Killed by the monster. I've known something like this would happen ever since that terrible business with the mate I was

building for it. Oh, if only I'd not trashed her like that. I don't know why it happened but there I was, getting on really well with the job, when I spotted those weird watery eyes and that great gormless face of his peering in at the window. Well, I just sort of flipped again. Of course, you-know-who went ballistic. He also said he would … 'be with me on my wedding night'! I wonder what he meant?

Victor

Dear Victor,

Sorry to hear about your chum. But why ever did you pull the plug on your project? Sometimes I do wonder about all you sad types who write to me. So often you have success within your reach only to throw it all away at the last moment! I'll never understand you lot! Then again, if people like you did have your acts together all the time you wouldn't be writing to people like me and then I'd be out of a job, wouldn't I? Ha ha ha!
Well, best of luck with the new wife,

Agatha

Dear Agatha,

I am done. My dearest Elizabeth is dead! Killed on our wedding night by the monster. I'd only nipped out for a mo and somehow it managed to sneak in and throttle her to death. Agatha! I made this monster so now I must find it and destroy it before it brings more sorrow to the world. Do you remember what I said about how my great discovery would make the world a better place for human beings? Ha ha. What a complete dim-wit I must have been!

Victor

Dear Victor,

Well, you knew what you were doing and now you've only got yourself to blame, haven't you? Surely you remember how I went out of my way to warn you of the consequences of such a foolhardy and irresponsible project the very first time you wrote to me? Oh dear, dear, dear! If only you'd taken my advice! Some people really do have such short memories!

Best wishes,

Agatha

DEAR AGAFFA,

I AM DOING A RUNNER. FRANKENSTEIN IS AFTER ME. HE IS TOOLED UP WITH SHOOTERS AND ALL KIND OF STUFF. I AM WHIZZING ACROSS THE FROZEN ICE HEADING TO NORTH POLE AND HE IS NOT FAR BEHIND ME! FIRST I'M AFTER HIM AND NOW HE'S AFTER ME!

IT'S A FUNNY OLD LIFE ISN'T IT, AGAFFA? BYE BYE! MUST DASH!

A. MONSTER

Dear A. Monster,

So you didn't go and punch a pillow after all! And now this Frankenstein chap has run out of patience with you! Well, now you're paying the price. Sometimes my job is so so frustrating. Why, oh why, don't you types just listen once in a while? Ah well, I suppose some people really are completely incapable of seeing an answer to a problem, even if it's as plain as the nose on their face!

Agatha

DEAR AGAFFA,

BOO HOO HOO! FRANKENSTEIN IS DEAD!
JUST AFTER WE'D PASSED A SHIP THAT WAS
STUCK IN THE ICE I NOTICED THAT HE
WASN'T CHASING ME ANY MORE SO I WENT
BACK TO SEE WHERE HE'D GOT TO. (WELL,
WHERE'S THE FUN IN A NICE CHASE IF NO
ONE'S CHASING YOU?) I WENT ON THE
SHIP AND THE DRIVER, WHO IS CALLED
CAPTAIN WALTON, TOLD ME THAT FRANK-
ENSTEIN HAS GONE TO MEET HIS MAKER
(SO I WONDER WHO MADE HIM, THEN?) ANY-
WAY, I WENT TO SEE HIS BODY AND SAY
GOODBYE TO HIM (I THINK I WILL MISS HIM
A LOT). BOO HOO. TALKING OF BODIES, I AM
A BIT OFF-COLOUR MYSELF AT THE MOMENT.
SORT OF YELLOWY GREEN ALL OVER WITH
SOME VERY YUKKY PURPLE AND
PINK SQUELCHY BITS. EVERY TIME
I SNEEZE SOME DRIBBLY GREY
STUFF COMES DOWN MY NOSETRILS.
I THINK IT'S MY BRAIN PUDDING. I
AM ALSO GETTING VERY SMELLY AND
MANY PARTS OF ME ARE DROPPING OFF ALL
OVER THE PLACE. I LOST ONE OF MY LEGS
YESTERDAY AND... OOPS THERE GOES
ANOTHER FINGER! I'VE ONLY GOT JUST
THESE TWO LEFT NOW SO IT IS GETTING
REALLY DIFFICULT TO WRITE THIS LET...
X T MLP N S. O E J S A O...

Dear A. Monster,

You types crease me up! You really do! Listen, luvvie. You might be upset over the death of this Frankenstein chap (though for the life of me I can't think why!) but there's no need to go to pieces like this! You really are going to have to pull yourself together. Will you do that for me, luvvie? Will you?

FANTASTIC FACTS 8: SCARY, SCARY, THAT'S OUR MARY! THE FRANKENSTEIN FACT FILE

1 Mary was only 18 years old when she wrote Frankenstein. She got the idea for the story in 1816 while she was on holiday with her boyfriend, Percy Shelley (the famous poet, whom she later married), the poet, Lord Byron and a doctor called John Polidori. Along with one or two other friends, they were staying at a posh villa on the shores of Lake Geneva in the Swiss mountains.

2 The weather was wet, cold and utterly miserable (well, it *was* their *summer* hol) so the chums were forced to spend loads of time indoors sitting by a blazing log fire, reading ghost stories and horror stories to keep themselves amused. After a while Lord Byron got a bit fed up and said something like, 'I know! Let's have a ripper competition to see who can write the scariest story. The tale that terrifies the togs off us will be the winner!'

3 The four chums all got to work straight away, each one racking their brain in order to come up with the most perfectly petrifying, pant-pulverizing plot. It's been said that to give themselves nightmares and therefore get lots of bizarre ideas for their spooky stories, they deliberately ate rotten meat – which should be taken with a pinch of salt (the rumour, not the meat).

4 As Mary hadn't done all that much writing before, she had quite a bit of difficulty getting going with her story and many days passed before she finally got inspired. Then, one dark and thundery night, as she was tossing and turning and generally having problems getting to sleep, she closed her eyes and immediately saw the scene that would become one of the most famous ones in the book. Yes ... just like that! In her mind's eye she saw a student kneeling beside the horrible 'phantasm' of a man which he had just put together. Seconds later she saw the 'thing' show signs of life and begin to move.

This vision seemed to come into her head from nowhere and she found it all really, really scary. She knew that if she could invent a story that frightened a reader as much as she'd been frightened she'd be on to a winner! All she needed to do was describe the horrible thing that 'haunted her pillow', as she put it. So she got cracking ... and the rest is her-story!

5 At around this time, all sorts of thrilling new scientific ideas were floating around and people were getting excited about robots and surgery and the recently discovered, newfangled stuff called electricity. One scientist called Galvani had used electricity to make the legs of a dead frog twitch and jerk as if the frog were coming back to life. Nowadays only an idiot would try and 'jump start' a frog, but we still talk of someone being '*galvanized*' into action when they are stimulated to do something. Galvani's nephew even tried using electricity to liven up the body of a murderer who'd recently been hanged. When he did, the dead murderer's jaw quivered and his left eye opened! All these things were obviously in Mary's mind when she was dreaming up the plot of her monstrous blockbuster.

6 In addition to calling her story *Frankenstein*, Mary gave it the posher-sounding subtitle of 'The Modern Prometheus'. Prometheus is a character in Greek mythology who, just like Victor, enjoyed cobbling together the odd home-made human being. He made his DIY people out of clay and stole fire from Heaven to help mankind. Just like Victor, poor old Prometheus ended up having a really bad time as a direct result of his body-bodging efforts. The god Zeus was so annoyed about them that he chained him to a rock and got an eagle to peck out great chunks of his liver.

7 *Frankenstein* was first published anonymously. In other words, when it came out as a book in 1818, no one had the foggiest idea who'd written the amazing story that was destined to become such a horrible success. When it was finally revealed that a *woman* had written it, everyone was gobsmacked! In those days, ladies were generally thought of as only being good for things like fainting and flower arranging. One astonished book critic said that if the story had been written by a man it would be 'excellent' but for a woman it was ... 'wonderful'! That's because they've got smaller brains than other people you know. (Book critics, that is, not women!)

8 In the original story Victor describes his creation as being 'beautiful' although (as *you* know) he was never keen on those weird eyes! After a while, the idea began to get about that the creature was generally rather repulsive and, by the time the story was turned into a stage play in 1823, everyone thought of it as the 'monster'. As a result, the actor who played Frankenstein's creation had to be given a really monstrous makeover. It was reported that such large amounts of make-up were used on his face that they turned his lips black and shrivelled up his skin. He was also said to have been left with a permanently gormless grin.

9 In 1931 a Hollywood film studio made a movie version of the Frankenstein story which turned out to be a blockbuster of its day *and* gave the monster the image that's stuck in people's minds ever since. In other words, the square-headed, bolt-in-the-neck, zipper-scarred little treasure that all horror movie fans know and love. The monster in the film was played by a handsome actor called William Henry Pratt – though you may know him better by his stage name, Boris Karloff. In order to get a few suitably horrible ideas and to prepare himself for the task of transforming dishy Boris into a complete dog's dinner, the make-up artist spent three months studying surgery. After his studies, he decided that in order to give someone a brain transplant, a surgeon would slice off the top of their head just like you slice off the top of a boiled egg (but would obviously resist the temptation to dip a bread 'soldier' in their scrummy brain juices).

He would then pop in the new brain, give the head a hinged 'lid' ... and clamp it shut! So now you know why the Frankenstein movie-monster has a flat-topped head. The metal peg or bolt in the monster's neck is supposed to be some sort of connection for the electricity that 'galvanizes' him into action (and is also really useful for hanging car keys on).

10 Some experts say that Frankenstein was the first ever science-fiction story. Others reckon it's one of the first real horror stories. Some of them say that the story is a sort of warning for future generations. Whenever anyone wants to talk about experiments where scientists are thought to be messing with nature just a bit too dangerously, they often use the word Frankenstein. Dolly the sheep, who was created in 1997 from a cell taken from a sheep's udder, has been described as a 'Frankenstein creation'. Things like the genetically modified tomatoes and cereals that have been in the news so much are frequently referred to as 'Frankenstein foods'. By describing these things in this way the critics are suggesting that too much interference with nature will probably have disastrous results for human beings in much the same way as Victor's meddlings with nature had terrible consequences for him and all the people around him. Baa, nonsense!

Finally, maybe you're wondering about the other stories that the fearsome foursome dreamed up? Well, the two super-poets, Byron and Shelley, got sort of bored with the whole lark after a while and didn't come up with anything remarkable but Doctor Polidori wrote a story called 'The Vampyre: A Tale', which is still *slightly* famous. Of course it's nowhere near as clever or brilliant or important as Mary's great story, which has led to so many hundreds of spin-off stories, movies, games, fancy dress costumes and masks and will no doubt keep bolt factories busy for years to come.

STORY 9: THE DUNWICH HORROR

Number nine in our Ten Best tales of terrific trepidation is a seriously scary story by the American horror writer, H P Lovecraft (1890–1937). Many of H P's tales are based on the idea that we humans aren't the only intelligent life forms wandering the world. That's right! There are some *other* extremely horrible, foul-smelling, non-human 'things' loose in our universe. The main desire of most of HP's ghastly 'creature-thing' creations is to inflict unspeakable pain and terror on all humans. Many of these ultra-scary, weird and dangerous monsters have been around for hundreds of thousands of years. And what's more, in addition to being deeply *evil*, they are often really, really, really ... *brainy*! The 'Dunwich Horror' (1928) is a story about just such a collection of inhuman terrors. It's set in a remote and forgotten corner of America at the beginning of the twentieth century and features the Whateley family ... particularly their extremely peculiar son, Wilbur. The Whateleys were a very odd bunch indeed. If you were unlucky enough to live just up the track from them you would probably be tempted to descibe them as 'the neighbours from hell'.

If you want to find out more about this gruesome mob, read on. But expect the worst! And don't say you haven't been warned!

THE NEIGHBOURS FROM HELL

This thing has been kept hushed up for too long! The world's got to know about it sooner or later! And that's why I've decided to go public with these extracts from my journals. I guess when people have read them, they'll say, 'More fool him... for going to live in a place like that!' But back in those days I was young and just starting out. Houses were cheap around those parts. And I needed some peace and quiet to begin work on my first horror novel. Dunwich looked like just the perfect spot for a young writer to kick off his career. (Well, that's what I thought at the time!) How was I to know my nearest neighbours would be ...

... THE WHATELEYS!

Extracts from the journals of Ezra T. Hopkin, novelist (retired)

October 1912

Moved into hilltop shack today. Home sweet home! This area really has got atmosphere. Hilly, with dark, bottomless ravines and smelly swamps. Ruined buildings and ancient stone circles everywhere! And hundreds of weird birds known as whip-poor-wills (after their haunting call). The locals are terrified of them. They believe they steal the souls of the dying. Also heard some spooky rumbling, groaning and hissing noises coming from beneath the biggest of the hills! All in all, this is a pretty gloomy spot, with a sinister air of foreboding everywhere. Perfect place for a budding horror writer ... like yours truly!

November 1912

Went into town for supplies and met some locals. What a bunch of odd-bods! So suspicious and sneaky looking! Like they'd got something to hide. Perhaps those rumours of devil worship, family violence and murder are true! (Only joking!)

January 1913

Saw my neighbours, the Whateleys, for the first time. I've a good view of their farmhouse down the valley from my place. What a weird pair! 'Old' Whateley's a real grizzled oldster. Spends most of his time studying ancient spell books and muttering gibberish. Looks at least half insane. Lavinia, his daughter, isn't much better. A most odd shape, with pink eyes, pink skin, and completely white

hair. Also chinless, like the old fellah! Think I've spotted her a few times already, wandering the hills during thunderstorms, reading those old spell books. Probably at least as barmy as the old man!

Early February 1913

Haven't slept a wink. All last night the most hideous screaming was coming from the Whateley place! So loud it even drowned out those rumblings from under the big hill and the constant barking of the local dogs. Whatever was happening?

Late February 1913

Found out what caused the screaming. It was Lavinia! She's had a baby! Not seen it yet.

Apparently they've called it Wilbur. No idea who the father is!

March 1913
Since baby 'Wilbur's' arrival I've noticed that Old Whateley has been buying rather a lot of cattle. But the odd thing is that their herd, which is in the field below my shack, doesn't seem to increase in size from its usual 11 or 12 beasts!

April 1913
Saw 'Wilbur' for the first time. Lavinia was carrying him through the pasture. He's a very big baby. Rather 'goat-like' in appearance. Poor kid!

May 1913
Fetched water from stream this morning. Noticed that the Whateley cattle all have wounds and dribbly sores on their bodies! Like they've been bitten?

June 1913
Passed Old Whateley and Lavinia on the track today. As I did I spotted two marks on Lavinia's neck. Exactly like the wounds I'd seen on the cattle!

Then spotted the same thing on the old man too! Maybe my imagination's running away with me? After all, I am a horror writer. Actually ... the horror novel's not going too well at the moment.

January 1914

 Saw Wilbur today. Now 11 months old, but is already able to talk – probably as well as a 15-year-old! Also getting his own 'look'. Yellowish skin, thick lips, coarse crinkly hair and long pointy ears. And completely chinless ... like Mom and Grandpop! Not the most beautiful of babies!

September 1914

Wilbur is now as large as a child of four. Spends a lot of time reading Old Whateley's magic books. Yesterday, I saw him standing in the middle of the stone circle on top of Sentinel hill (the big one where the noises come from). Enormous old spell book open in his arms and screaming, 'Yog-Sothoth! Yog-Sothoth!' at the top of his voice. Very disturbing. Gave me a bad attack of goosebumps! Probably some childish prank though. Horror novel hardly going at all now. Spending all my time watching Whateleys. Sort of becoming an obsession.

October 1914

Old Whateley is building an enormous extension on the farmhouse. Without windows! Wonder why? Re. horror novel: no progress at all. Not written a word for ages!

May 1915

Keep seeing young Wilbur wandering the neighbourhood muttering and chanting to himself (often in rhyme). He's got a problem with the local dogs. They can't stand him and have tried to kill him several times. You're not going to believe this, but ... his mother now insists that he carry a large pistol to defend himself!

1917

Wilbur is now four and a half. His voice has begun to break and a crop of stubble is sprouting from his cheeks (and what passes for his chin). I spoke to Earl Sawyer, the neighbourhood cattle trader, yesterday. He says that he called to deliver some fresh cows to the Whateleys earlier and smelt the most dreadful stench coming from their new extension. I've also been chatting to our local door-to-door pedlar. He spent a few minutes in the Whateley's kitchen the other morning. He thinks he heard a horse (!) stamping about in the room above.

1 August 1924

Woken at dawn by great shrieking and moaning of whip-poor-wills. Looked out to see hundreds of them gathered around the Whateley place. Most odd!

2 August 1924

Have been into town, picking up on gossip. Now I know the reason for the bird chorus. Old Whateley died yesterday! Amongst his last words to Wilbur, he is said to have croaked, 'Yew grows ... and that grows faster!' and, 'Feed it reg'lar, Willy!' Whatever could he mean? Re. horror novel: have more or less abandoned it now.

Halloween 1926

Mrs Whateley has disappeared! Oddly enough she spoke to me only last week. And more than just the usual couple of words. She seemed very upset and quite desperate to talk to someone. Told me that she had become 'afraid' of Wilbur.

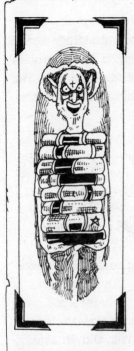

Summer 1927

Have just seen Wilbur for the first time in months! Hardly recognized him. Can't believe how he's grown. He must be over 7 feet tall and looks even more 'goat-like' than ever. Local gossips say he's been very busy with those old magic books. He's been visiting lots of libraries and universities, looking for some ancient text called the Necronomicon, written by the mad Arab, Abdul Alhazred. Says he must have it! Still no sign of Mrs Whateley.

Winter 1927/8

Had a trip to the city the other day and bumped into Dr Armitage, my old professor from Miskatonic College. Told him about my life in the hills and my strange 14-year-old neighbour, Wilbur. What a coincidence! Dr A. has just had a visit from him! (Well, they say truth's weirder than fiction, don't they!) Wilbur wanted to take away the college's copy of the Necronomicon but Dr A. refused. He now senses that Wilbur isn't prepared to take 'no' for an answer. Fears that something terrible may happen.

July 1928

I've had a letter from Dr Armitage. He's doing some sort of study of the people in the Dunwich area and has asked me to spend some time at Miskatonic next month to help with his research. Quite looking forward to it.

August 1928

Am at Miskatonic with Dr A. Something really terrible has happened! A couple of nights ago I was woken by wild barking from the savage college guard-dog. Closely followed by a scream so awful that it will haunt my dreams for ever. I leapt from my bed and raced to the library, where the sounds had come from! Dr Armitage and a couple of professors had got there before me. One had fainted on the spot, so terrible was the scene before us. I'm going to describe it but first I must warn anyone who is troubled by nightmares or nervousness to read no further.

Lying there, twitching helplessly in a pool of stinking yellow ooze was the 'thing'. It was at least 9 feet tall and had the goat-like, chinless face of Wilbur Whateley! Apart from that, it was not human. This was plain to see because much of its clothing had been torn away by the college guard-dog which now had its huge paws resting on the thing's shuddering, jerking chest. From its stomach there dangled a mass of greenish-grey tentacles. Each one had a red sucking mouth. The skin above the thing's waist was scaly like an alligator's, but below it was covered in black fur. A sort of trunk stuck out from its lower back with some kind of mouth or throat on the end. On each of the hips was something that looked like an eye. The legs themselves were like the legs of a prehistoric reptile ending in a half-hoof, half-claw shape.

As the thing squirmed and thrashed, sounds came from its mouth, like, 'Yog-Sothoth, Yog-Sothoth', but it was hard to tell because of the sudden outbreak of shrieking from hundreds of whip-poor-wills outside. Then it stopped twitching and the dog threw back its head and howled. Ten minutes later the police arrived but by now all there was left of the 'thing' was some sticky white powder on the library floor.

1 September, 1928

Have returned to my shack. The university men and I have vowed to tell no one about what we saw at the library. Back here at Dunwich the terrible stench from the deserted Whateley place increases each day. And yesterday I heard a weird 'lapping' noise coming from down there. The local dogs won't stop barking and the cattle stamp and bellow constantly. They're all being driven mad with fear! But by what?

9 September, 1928 (a.m.)

The wooden boards of that big extension at the Whateley place have been shattered like a bomb has hit them. Something terrible has broken out of there! This morning one of the local farmers found half his cows gone while the rest were on their knees, groaning in agony, with at least half their blood sucked out.

9 September 1928 (p.m.)

Whatever awful thing has burst loose on the world seems to have gone into the big ravine next to the Whateley place. A boy says he's seen huge footprints in the mud. Everyone's terrified and barricading themselves in their houses for the night.

10 September 1928 (a.m.)

I'm really scared. Sometime last night something horrible happened at the Frye's farm. At midnight their neighbour got a phone call from Mrs Frye. She was shrieking hysterically, saying something like, 'Oh gawd help us ... it's out there...!' but then her voice was drowned out by hideous screaming followed by a huge crash. Then the line went dead.

First thing this morning a gang of boys and men went up to the Frye place. They found bloodied cow parts all over the fields and maimed and dying cattle everywhere. There was no sign of the Fryes. Their home was completely wrecked with a horrible yellow tarry stickiness on the ground and the air was filled with the most terrible smell. I don't think we'll ever see them again.

10 September 1928 (p.m.)

I've heard from Dr Armitage. Just after the terrible events at the university he found Wilbur's diary in the library. Ever since then he's been trying to make sense of the strange scrawlings and jottings in it. He says he's just made some sort of breakthrough, but will not tell me what. All he will say is that what he has discovered is most terrible and that there is some sort of danger to all of mankind. He seems almost paralysed with fear.

11 September, 1928

I have just been through the most terrifying day of my life. After what I have seen I do not think that I will ever be completely normal again. I will write this entry, then I must rest for a long time. At noon today Dr Armitage arrived in Dunwich, looking grim and determined. He had with him a container of powdered chemicals. He asked me and some of the other villagers to take him to the Frye farm. When we got there we found the car belonging to the policemen who'd come to investigate the disappearance. It was empty. The last time the officers had been seen they'd been on their way into the big ravine. Pale and shaking, Old Sam Hutchins was just telling us how he'd warned them not to go down there when Earl Sawyer came running up, looking like he would die from fear! He was yelling, 'It's out! It's out!' Then he babbled something about how there'd been a great swishing and squelching from the ravine and next moment all the trees were waving and bending like in a great storm and the air had been filled with a terrible smell.

Whatever it was that had come out of the ravine was now making its way to the ancient stone circle so we all ran to Sentinel Hill as fast as we could. When we got there Dr Armitage handed me his binoculars and told me to stay put and observe. Then he disappeared into the trees. Five minutes later I spotted him near the stone circle. Then I heard a sound that made my heart jump to my throat and my blood turn to ice. It was a deafening, croaking roar of 'Yog-Sothoth

Yog-Sothoth' ... the very words I had heard Wilbur yell all that time ago. At that moment I got my first sight of what would later become known as 'The Dunwich Horror'!

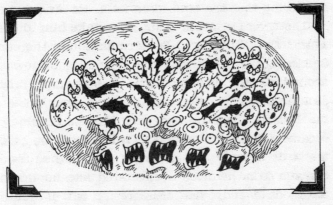

It was bigger than any living thing I'd ever imagined and seemed to be made from a mass of squirming tentacles. But as I focused the binoculars, I saw that this monstrous creature was covered all over with hideous bulging eyes, gaping mouths and lashing trunks. And most horrible of all ... on the end of each trunk was ... a face! A face I recognized immediately. Each of those leering, drooling, goat-like apparitions was ... a Whateley!

Croaking and bleating and swishing, the nightmare monstrosity slowly advanced on Dr Armitage who was frantically scattering the white powder from the container and chanting some sort of rhyme which I couldn't make out. Just as the horrendous thing reached down to enfold him in those lashing tentacles and suck the life from him, a great bolt of lightning shot from the sky to the altar stone at the centre of the circle. It was followed by a scream so terrifying and ear-shattering that the binoculars fell from my hands. By the time I'd picked them up and focused them again, the thing and Dr Armitage were gone. Suddenly the trees and grass and undergrowth around me and the others were whipped into a fury as a great stench of death and decay swept down the hillside. Dogs howled and the sky above us became filled with whip-poor-wills. Next moment the birds began to fall to earth, screaming as they did, and soon the fields were littered with hundreds of the dead and dying creatures. It felt as if the world was ending. But eventually all went quiet and the only sound that broke the silence was the occasional wail of a half-dead whip-poor-will.

A few moments later Dr Armitage appeared from the trees at the bottom of the hill.

'It is destroyed for ever,' he said quite calmly. 'Just as Wilbur grew, it grew. But it grew far faster. And like him, it was not a thing of the normal world! The Whateleys raised it so it could play its terrible part in the things that were to come. But now ... it is no more.'

'W-w-where did it come from?' I gasped.

'It was Wilbur's twin brother,' whispered Dr Armitage. 'But it looked much more like their father than he did!'

FANTASTIC FACTS 9: BORN TO SCARE

Loads of fear fans reckon that HP Lovecraft is the bee's knees (or the loathsome *thing's* scaly, dripping tentacles) as far as modern horror writing is concerned. His strange and scary stories have had a *massive* influence on dozens of film makers and horror writers (including the mega-successful, Stephen King). In fact, poor old HP only managed to get *one* book published during his short and troubled life but since his death, in 1937, his career has *really* taken off! His stories have been published over and over again, they've been translated into twelve languages and more than *twenty* of them have been made into movies! There's a huge HP Lovecraft fan club with websites on the internet, and masses of board and computer games inspired by his brilliantly scary ideas.

So, what sort of person do you have to be and what sort of things have to happen to you in order to become one of the most influential supernatural and horror story writers of the twentieth century?

HOW TO BE A HORRENDOUSLY SUCCESSFUL HORROR WRITER: THE LOVECRAFT FILES

1 Make an early start with your education.

HP, who was born in 1890, was a shy but brainy little lad. He could recite poetry by the time he was two and read by the time he was three.

"FRANKENSTEIN BY MARY SHELLEY..."

2 Get a pseudonym.

After reading the Arabian Nights, HP decided to give himself a pseudonym (or pen name). This is something that many writers do. But not usually when they're five! That's how old HP was when he decided to call himself ... wait for it! ... Abdul Alhazred!

3 Have a helpful grandad – with a weird name.

When he was growing up, HP spent a lot of time with his grandfather, Whipple Van Buren Phillips. Whipple loved to tell little HP horror stories.

4 Get bamboozled by your mum.

It's reported that HP's mum was fond of telling him what an ugly child he was. (Must have worked wonders for the little chap's self-confidence!) And, just to make sure that he was completely baffled about how he fitted into the world, i.e. which loo he should visit, which changing room to use at the local swimming baths ... she told him that he was a girl! She even kitted him out in dresses and stuff until he was about six!

5 Get out less.

Probably as a result of all his mum's tender loving care, HP never felt like getting out much, even when he was a teenager. While all the other young fellahs were out clubbing and chatting up the birds, he stayed at home. However, he did finally pluck up the courage to spend a night away from home. At the tender age of thirty-two!

6 Be original in your choice of meeting places.

When HP eventually got round to getting his first proper girlfriend, his favourite place to meet her was the local graveyard. How romantic! Just him, and her, and the headstones!

7 Have some really powerful 'pet' hates.

HP is said to have absolutely detested dogs, movies, seafood and all alcoholic drinks.

8 Recognize that you are somehow 'different'.

HP knew that he 'didn't fit' all that comfortably into the times he lived in. However, it didn't bother him too much because he always had the weird and exciting world of his imagination to escape into. He said, 'I am an outsider. Everything I love has been dead for two centuries.' He wasn't completely isolated and did have a few good friends who admired and supported him. Sadly though, when he died, only four people attended his funeral.

9 Follow your dreams.
HP is said to have got tons of his great story ideas from his dreams. In order to be able to remember them, he always made sure he wrote them down (not while he was actually having them though).

10 Make contact with the forces from beyond (maybe).
Amongst HP Lovecraft's army of fans there are some who believe that he didn't actually imagine his characters and places. They think that all the weird things and strange worlds he wrote about really do exist! They reckon the reason HP knew so much about them was because he was an extremely sensitive, 'fine tuned' sort of person – almost like a super-powerful TV satellite dish that is able to pick up broadcasts and messages that ordinary receivers can't get.

Of course, there are many other Lovecraft fans who think this is utter twaddle and that he was just extra-brilliant at dreaming up ripping horror yarns filled with extra-bizarre creations like the Dunwich Horror and the four odious monstrosities you're about to meet. It would have taken a whole book to tell you about all of his scary beings but this bevy of beauties should keep you in nightmares for months to come:

LOVECRAFT'S LOVELIES

Cthulhu is part dragon, part octopus and part human. It's got a grotesque, scaly, rubbery body with long narrow wings, and a pulpy octopus-like head with tentacles. Its face is a mass of feelers. On its front and back feet it has gigantic claws. You can meet this adorable great mutt in the 'The Call Of Cthulhu' (1926).

The Deep Ones start off as children but they gradually mutate into creatures that are part fish, part human. They're mainly a greyish-green colour but have white bellies. Their bodies are like an ape's or a human's, but their heads are more fish-like. They have webbed paws, bulging eyes and pulsating gills in their necks. They move by hopping around, either on two legs or four, and communicate in croaks and howls. Cuddle up to one in 'The Shadow Over Innsmouth' (1931).

Ghouls are part dog, part human. Most of the time they walk around on two legs with a forward slumping movement. They have a body texture that is rubbery. In  the story, 'Pickman's Model' (1926), we meet one with a 'doggish' face – glaring, bloodshot eyes, a flat nose, slobbering lips and pointed ears. Its enormous body is 'caked in mould' and its feet are 'half-hooved'. In its bony claws it's holding a half-eaten man. As it crouches, shiftily watching for its next victim, it gnaws the man's head, in exactly the same way that you or I might nibble at a chocolate bar!

Night Gaunts fly around 'clutching' at things! They have smooth, oily surfaces (like the skin of whales), unpleasant, inward-curving horns, half-formed paws, bat wings and barbed tails that lash  around constantly. They're a bit like humans but they never laugh or smile … mainly because they haven't got an actual face to laugh or smile with! Just a 'suggestion' of one where their face ought to be. Face up to them in 'The Dream-Quest of Unknown Kadath' (1926).

Sweet dreams!

STORY 10: DRACULA

The story that fills the final slot in our hideously horrendous line-up is one of the most famous horror stories of all time: *Dracula* (1897) by Bram Stoker (1847–1912). Bram is said to have thought of it after having a midnight supper with a Hungarian professor who could speak twenty languages and was an expert on all things weird. The Prof told Bram about a horrible fifteenth-century ruler called Vlad the Impaler who liked to spike his enemies on huge wooden stakes then watch them die in agony

Bram Stoker

while he ate his dinner. If any of his dinner guests complained they were also given a piece of 'stake' for their next course! After this, Bram had a nightmare (are you surprised?) about a vampire king rising from his tomb. He then wrote the story, turning Vlad into Dracula and the Prof into a slightly different Prof.

The story has been in print for over a hundred years and has been adapted for films, TV, comics, theatre and radio, over and over again. It's a grim and gloomy tale so maybe it would be a good idea to finish our top ten on a cheerful note by turning it into an all-singing, all-dancing musical spectacular!

"**The Great Vein Drain**"
A DRACULA SPECTACULAR
Cast

Jonathan Harker (Solicitor's clerk)

Count Dracula

The Three Brides of Dracula

Wolves

Mina (Jonathan's girlfriend)

Lucy (Mina's friend)

Dr Seward

Quincey Morris (Lucy's friends)

Lord Godalming (Lucy's fellah)

Professor Van Helsing (Weirdness expert specializing in Vampires)

At tonight's performance the role of the "chorus" will be sung by the three Brides of Dracula.

Scene one: The entrance to Castle Dracula. Solicitor's clerk, Jonathan Harker, is being welcomed by Count Dracula. He is there to help the Count sort out his purchase of a house in England.

Dracula: *Welcome to Transylvania,*
In the country of Romania.
Please enter Castle Drac'.
(You'll make a tasty snack.)

Harker: *What a night! What a night!*
I'm dying for a bite!

Dracula: *Well that sort of thing,*
Is just up my street!

Harker: *Yes, I'd love a bite ... to eat!*

Chorus: *He'd love a bite to eat!*
He'd love a bite to eat!

Scene two: During a daytime wander around the castle, Jonathan discovers some earth-filled wooden boxes. He opens one ... and gets a shock!

Harker: *This terrible sight,*
          Has given me a fright!
          It's the spooky old Creep.
          He seems fast asleep,
          But he's lying in some mould!
          And his skin is icy cold!
          And he looks very ill.
          Plus his heart is quite still,
          So with this coffin for his bed,
          I fear he must be ... DEAD!
          I'm sure he can't be faking!
          And I've just started sh-sh-shaking!

Dracula: *The fool is quite mistaken.*
          For tonight I will awaken!
          I haven't passed away.
          I'm just sleeping through the day!
          I must lay here in the gloom.
          Or I will meet my doom.
          Of daylight I am frightened.
          I cannot be enlightened.
          If I didn't work the night-shift,
          My destruction would be quite swift!

Scene three: Some time later Jonathan sees the Count slowly crawling down the sheer face of the castle wall. He now realizes that the Count is very weird and that he (Jonathan) may be in some trouble.

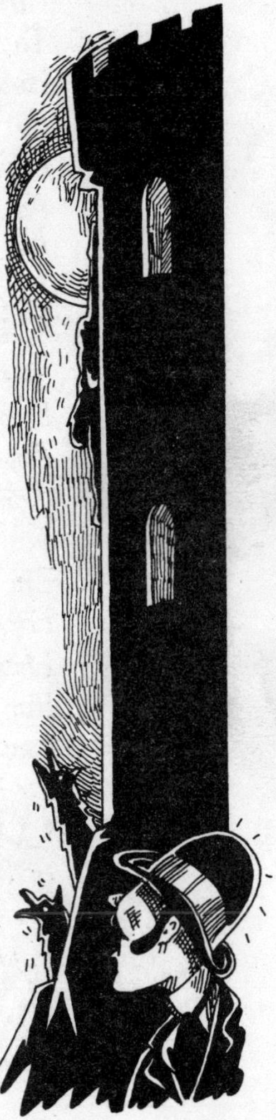

Harker:
But how can he crawl
Down a vertical wall?
To do a thing like that
He must be part bat!

Dracula:
I am that and more.
I'm mad on fresh gore!

Wolves:
He's incredibly savage.
He tells us who to ravage.
He's the leader of the pack!
We all love good old Drac.

Brides:
And we love him too.
Cos our necks he does chew.

1st Bride: *Blood's his fave drinky.*

2nd Bride: *So we all think he's dinky.*

3rd Bride: *And not the slightest bit kinky.*

Chorus:
We all think he's dinky!
Not the slightest bit kinky!

Scene four: The Count imprisons Jonathan in the castle, then leaves for England with his earth-filled boxes.

Dracula: *I'm off for my vacation,*
To a tea-drinking nation.
But I'll not drink one cup,
On fresh blood I'll sup.
Here you will remain,
And my brides will 'entertain'.
Bye girls!

Brides: *So long, sucker!*

Harker: *From this fiend in a cape.*
I've just got to escape.
I must try with persistence,
For I don't want to Romania
For the rest of my existence!

Chorus: *He don't want to Romania*
For the rest of his existence!

Scene five: A spooky ship loaded with boxes of earth drifts into Whitby harbour in the North of England, then runs aground. Its dead captain is tied to the wheel and there's no sign of the crew anywhere. A large wolf-like creature leaps ashore then bounds off in the direction of the clifftop churchyard.

Policeman: *What a palaver,*
The captain's a cadaver!

1st carter: *And did you see that creature's*
Bloodstained fangy features.

2nd carter: *Now we're all of a quiver,*
For the boxes we must deliver.

Scene six: Jonathan's girlfriend, Mina, happens to be staying in Whitby with her best friend Lucy. One night, Lucy sleepwalks her way to the clifftop churchyard. Mina follows and witnesses a strange en-Count-er.

Mina: *Those eyes so red and skin so white.*
It is a creature of the night!
Lucy, Lucy!

Dracula: *All nice and juicy!*

Lucy: *Ooh me throat! It's gone all goosey!*

Chorus: *Ooh 'er throat! It's gone all goosey!*
Ooh 'er throat! It's gone all goosey!

Scene seven: Not long afterwards Lucy becomes ill. She's often pale and tired. No matter how many blood transfusions she receives from the friends that have gathered round to help her she continues to deteriorate.

Godalming: *Heavens above!*
You look terrible, love.

Doctor: *All wobbly and pale.*
And ever so frail!

Lucy: *I feel terribly pained.*
And ever so drained!

Professor: *That's the fourth fill-up she's had this week!*

Morris: *Perhaps she's sprung a leak?*

Chorus: *Perhaps she's sprung a leak?*
Perhaps she's sprung a leak!

Scene eight: Despite all their efforts the plucky pals are unable to save Lucy. The bloodsucker took her. She dies and is buried near Hampstead Heath. A few days later small children begin disappearing on the Heath but are found later wandering around with small puncture marks on their necks. They say they have been with the nice 'bloofer' lady.

Professor: *On the necks of these tots,*
            There are tiny blood clots.

Doctor: *By some fiend they've been smitten,*
            Then viciously bitten.

Morris: *Somewhere on this Heath…*

Godalming: *Lurks a ghoul with big teeth!*

Scene nine: The beautiful lady turns out to be Lucy! After all Drac's attacks she has become one of the undead! The chaps have no alternative but to open up her coffin and put a stop to her hanky panky once and for all!

Professor: *Stick in the stake! Then give it a thrust.*

Godalming: *I'm not awf'ly keen. But I will if I must.*
           I'll do it right quick. Just under her bust!

Lucy: *Oi, mind that sticker. SPLATT!*
            Ooh me ticker!

Godalming: *Quick. Fetch the vicar!*

Scene ten: Drac strikes back by turning his attentions to Mina. She too, begins to fall under his spell.

Dracula: *I've come from Transylvania,*
               Of your blood I want to drain yer.

Mina: *Oh, what the heck,*
               Have a bite of me neck!
               I'm a sucker for Vampire-mania!

Dracula: *The blood it is oozing. It's time to get boozing!*

Chorus: *The blood it is oozing. It's time to get boozing!*

208

Scene eleven: But it isn't too late to save Mina. Jonathan (who has escaped from Castle Dracula) gets together with the others. They work out that the Count has had the wooden boxes delivered to various spots around the country so that he will have plenty of handy '*overday*' stopping places. They trace the coffins then make them useless to him by bunging holy wafers in each of them.

Professor: *He's a pain in the neck!*
             So his plans we will wreck.

Doctor: *Have no fear.*
             The magic biccies are here!

Harker: *But what about your trick.*
             With the stinky garlic?

Doctor: *It's safer with a wafer!*

Professor: *We must not miss one. We just cannot risk it!*

Morris: *Well I thought I'd seen all. But this takes the*
             biscuit!

Dracula: *But they did miss a coffin,*
             And now I am loffin',
             Cos that is the coffin,
             They've carried me off in!
             Ha, ha, ha, ha, … HA!

Chorus: *And that is the coffin.*
             They've carried him off in!

Scene twelve: The Count has himself shipped back to Transylvania. The fearless friends pursue him. Just as he is about to re-enter his castle they stop the wagon carrying his coffin and Jonathan sets about him with a big knife.

Harker: *Evil Count Dracula,*
               I am going to tackle yer,
               I'll cut off yer noggin',
               To put a stop to yer snoggin',
               And then, my dear Mina,
               Will feel a lot cleaner.
               It'll end yer blood lust
               And turn yer to dust!

Chorus: *With one clean sweep,*
               That's made us weep.
               He's stopped his blood lust,
               And turned him to dust!

Harker: *Now it's your turn, toxic teeth!*

Chorus: *See you later, Vampire haters.*

Rest: *In a while, croccy smiles!*

210

FANTASTIC FACTS 10: SOME DAFT FANGS PEOPLE ASK ABOUT VAMPIRES

1 WHAT IS A VAMPIRE?

Vampires are human beings who are neither dead nor alive. That is why they are often referred to as the 'undead'. They do not eat food like we do, but depend entirely on fresh blood which they suck from other human beings. They spend their days hidden away in coffins, then come out at night and wander around looking for victims (or trying to remember where they hid their false teeth).

2 WHERE DO YOU FIND VAMPIRES?

They pop up all over the place! Graveyards, books, spooky forests, movies, old buildings, cricket matches, bedrooms, toy shops ... everywhere really! Lots of people think that vampires mostly hang about in Transylvania in Romania in Eastern Europe, but they've been turning up all over the world for thousands of years! Vampires are mentioned in ancient legends from places as far apart as Africa, China, India and South America.

Editor's note: Sorry, we were wrong about the cricket matches, that's umpires!

3 HOW DO YOU BECOME A VAMPIRE?

a) Get bitten by a vampire. If this happens enough times, and the vampire manages to slurp down most of your blood, you too will become a vampire (or just *very* pale).

b) Peasants in various countries used to believe that if a person, animal or bird jumped or flew over a freshly dead body then that body would become a vampire. So, try to avoid dying whilst competing in the 100-metre hurdles, feeding the pigeons or frolicking with giant kangaroos.

c) Another way to become a vampire is to have your shadow stolen. This usually happens when you are standing next to a building. Whilst you are looking elsewhere, someone sneaks up and nails your shadow to the wall. Then you walk off without it, not even hearing the horrible tearing sound as you part company with it or noticing that it's gone! Therefore: stay away from walls, check your shadow regularly and keep it with you at *all* times!

4 WHAT CAN I DO TO PREVENT BEING ATTACKED BY VAMPIRES?

a) Surround yourself with garlic. Vampires just *hate* the smell of garlic. (Have you ever seen a vampire in an Italian restaurant?) Rub garlic on all the windows, doors and bedheads in your house. That way you will never be visited by vampires (or anyone else for that matter). When you go out, hang a necklace of garlic bulbs around your neck (but prepare to be approached by people wishing to buy interesting cooking ingredients).

b) Hide silver knives under the mattresses in your house. (Ask your family to spread their butter with their fingers.)

c) Scatter lots of seeds and salt around your house. But expect the mice to ask if you ever do cheesy wotsits!

d) Turn your shoes around before you go to bed. Remember to take them off first.

e) Place a mirror by your bedroom door. Vampires hate *them* too! This may be something to do with the fact that they don't have a reflection and are therefore never able to check if their hair is tidy and their teeth looking nice and sharp.

5 WHAT CAN I DO IF I AM ACTUALLY ATTACKED BY A VAMPIRE?

There are lots of things you can do. The most sensible and deeply satisfying one is to hide behind a teacher.

Failing that, why not try:

a) Waving a crucifix at the vampire. They hate them and usually run off. If this doesn't work, try pushing the crucifix up the vampire's nose.

b) Thrusting a thorn under the vampire's tongue. Oddly enough, many of the people who recommend this traditional anti-vampire trick have less than the normal number of fingers.

c) Wafting a Eucharistic wafer at the vampire. This is a special, holy sort of biscuit. Make sure you get the proper kind. Ordinary biscuits like chocolate digestives and pop tarts are useless. The vampire will see through them straight away. Especially if they're coconut rings!

As a last resort you could always try biting the vampire back. These bullying types don't like to get a taste of their own medicine. (They much prefer *your* blood!)

214

6 HOW WOULD I DESTROY A VAMPIRE FOR EVER?

Withering sarcasm has no effect on vampires. What you need to do is get very physical with them. Try driving a wooden stake through their heart for starters. Make sure it's the right kind of wood, though. Your dad's old toothpick will not do. Use wood from an ash, oak or hawthorn tree. And when you finally ram in the stake, give it a really good thrust. Don't be surprised to hear the vampire shriek. (Vampires have feelings too, you know!)

Just to make entirely sure that the vampire is out of action for good, cut out its heart and burn it. Then scatter the ashes on water. Preferably in a river. If you do put them down the toilet make sure you flush it at least three or four times and give the bowl a really thorough clean, maybe followed by a rinse with some holy water.
USEFUL TIP: Before trashing the vampire throw a shroud over it. This will prevent its blood splashing all over you and possibly turning you into a vampire too.
IMPORTANT WARNING: Whilst destroying the vampire do not bottle out half-way through the job. There's nothing worse than a half-dead undead. They're about a thousand times more dangerous than the normal sort.

7 HOW DO I RECOGNIZE A VAMPIRE?

Vampires vary in appearance. Sometimes they transform themselves into wolves, cats, bats or wisps of mist and smoke. This makes things a bit difficult as many people will think you've flipped your lid if they see you waving crucifixes at passing patches of fog, or hurling cloves of garlic at next door's ginger tom.

Of course, if the vampire has its mouth open, you'll probably recognize it by its long pointed teeth, but by then it will probably be too late as it will already be sinking them into your throat!

One sure way of spotting a vampire is by their smell. They stink to high heaven! And so would you if you'd spent the last 3,000 years sharing a rotting coffin with 6,000 earthworms and drinking nothing but other people's blood. Do not make the mistake of thinking that all smelly people are vampires though. Some of them may just be a couple of deodorants short of personal freshness. You can also recognize vampires by the fact that they do not have shadows.

8 WHAT'S A VAMPIRE BAT?

Vampire bats are the pesky little critters that are so closely associated with vampires. They're much, much fiercer than other sorts of bats and are incredibly strong for their size. Like vampires, they only come out at night and hate any kind of light. They look like miniature gargoyles and have needle sharp fangs and long pointed pink tongues (just one each). They're found in Central and South America and mainly attack cows and horses.

OI!.... WHO DO YOU THINK YOU'RE CALLING A GARGOYLE !

Good news: attacks on humans are rare. Bad news: when they do attack people, they bite their toes, the tips of their ears and their faces! Uuurgh! Once the blood is flowing they don't suck it like proper vampires are supposed to do but lap it like your cat laps milk from a saucer. All right, so you've not got a cat! In which case they lap at it like your *grandad* laps *tea* from a saucer!

9 IS FEAR OF VAMPIRES COMMON?

Yes, especially amongst people who're daft enough to believe in them! A Polish man called Demetrious Myicura was completely vampire bats! Or, to put it another way, he was so terrified of being attacked by a vampire that it became an obsession with him. In 1973, he was found dead in his flat in Stoke-on-Trent. Had a vampire finally got him? No! A pickled onion had! Well, that's what the police thought before they found out about his fear of vampires and discovered that the bowls of garlic and salt (mixed with his own wee!) at all the doorways of his flat were all vampire deterrents. Just to be sure that he was completely vampire-proof Demetrious also liked to go to bed with a garlic clove in his mouth. The police had found the garlic clove (or 'pickled onion', as they call them in Stoke) lodged in his throat. He'd choked to death on it (maybe during a vampire nightmare?).

THAT MR MYICURA! HE MUST DO A LOT OF COOKING! HE SPENDS A FORTUNE ON GARLIC!

...AND SALT!

10 IS THERE ANY PROOF THAT REAL VAMPIRES DO EXIST?
Well, *you'll* have to be the judge of that. Read the evidence, then decide for yourself!

THE CASE OF ARNOLD PAOLE – A REAL LIVE VAMPIRE?

THE EVIDENCE FOR
In the early eighteenth century, European newspapers were full of the story of Arnold Paole. In 1731 the Austrian government had sent an investigating surgeon to a village in Serbia after locals reported a number of suspicious deaths in the area. They blamed them on a man called Arnold Paole. But Arnold had died five years earlier! People reckoned he was regularly nipping out of his coffin of an evening and sucking up to old pals, not to mention a few strangers.

The surgeon ordered Arnold's grave to be opened and his body was found to be in perfect, *undecomposed* condition! Oower! Even more weird and gruesome, his eyes were filled with blood! And blood was gushing from his ears and nose! And despite the fact that his fingernails and toenails had dropped off, new ones had grown in their place!

OH... HELLO...! I DON'T SUPPOSE YOU'VE GOT ANY NAIL SCISSORS ON YOU, HAVE YOU ??!

To put a stop to Arnold's alleged vampiring, a stake was driven through his heart. As it went in he was said to have given a loud groan, after which huge amounts of blood spurted from his body!

Can you take any more? You can! OK, we'll go on...

Arnold was said to have attacked cattle as well as people. His people victims had had the anti-vampire treatment but others had eaten meat from the cattle and they too had become undead! Fifteen graves were opened up and eleven of the bodies showed signs of being preserved by their own night-time blood-sucking activities. One woman, who'd been buried for 90 whole days, was reported to have been much fatter than she had been when she died!

So what do you make of all that then? Makes your blood run dry, doesn't it?

And what became of those cows he'd attacked, the ones that hadn't been eaten? The thought of 'undead' Daisys and Buttercups, flitting around graveyards, their eyes glowing red and their great fangs glistening in the moo-nlight, is just too horrible to think about, isn't it?

THE EVIDENCE AGAINST

While people in eighteenth century Europe were waiting for education-for-everyone to be invented, they passed the time by believing tons of utter twaddle, like:

GOOSE POO'S A GREAT HAIR RESTORER.

KEEP A BAT BONE IN YOUR CLOTHES AND YOU'LL BE LUCKY.

PUT A BAT'S EYE IN YOUR POCKET AND YOU'LL GO INVISIBLE.

IF YOU'VE GOT CHOLERA, SLEEP IN A CHURCH-YARD, THEN YOU'LL GET BETTER.

...and oodles of similar claptrap. Even brainy bods like doctors didn't know about stuff like bacteria and microbes and that it's not a good idea to lick your fingers after sticking them up the bottom of a plague victim who's been dead for 16 weeks. What everyone *did* know though, was that dead bodies were linked with nasty stuff like illness and bad smells (remember that vampire pong!), usually followed by *yet more* dead bodies!

REALLY INTERESTING BUT HORRIBLE BIT: DO NOT READ!
Here's some stuff about dead bodies that we know *now* but they didn't know *then*! It may help you make up your mind about vampires. Or just make you throw up...

a) The skin of a corpse shrinks, making the hair look as if it's grown.

b) Gases form in rotting bodies which cause them to make noises which could easily be mistaken for moans and groans. Baked bean fans will know all about this.

c) If a stake is driven into a corpse these gases can cause it to sit up and let out a noise that sounds just like a shriek. Sort of a GERROFF-THWAARP-SQUEEEK! noise.

d) The decaying blood in a dead body sometimes expands, then leaks from the mouth and eyes and ears. (By the way, what are you having for tea tonight?)

e) Decay sometimes causes dead bodies to swell up. (Hmmmm ... *sausages*. Nice!)

f) When toenails and fingernails have dropped off corpses, the spaces where they were often look like new nails. (Sausages with crisps ... even better!)

Beginning to get the picture? Now consider this!

g) People who were bitten by animals with rabies often behaved oddly, then died!

h) People who suffer from the illness known as porphyria are often pale, sensitive to sunlight, and allergic to garlic!

i) Historians have noticed that vampire scares often happened at the same time as epidemics of deadly diseases like bubonic plague or cholera. In other words *terrifying* and *upsetting* times with people popping their clogs right, left and centre and no one having the faintest idea what's going on due to them all being completely ignorant.

So, making up stories about vampires may well have been people's way of trying to explain lots of sad and scary, weird stuff they didn't understand. Or maybe not?

NOW! YOU MUST MAKE YOUR DECISION

If you're not already there, why not retire to your bedchamber and give this matter your careful consideration. But leave the light on while you do and keep a bulb of garlic and a sharpened stake handy ... just in case! Night night. Sleep tight. Mind the vampires don't bite.

EPILOGUE

Blood satisfactorily chilled? Stomach nicely churned? Spine suitably tingled? Hair turned completely white overnight? Good! You've obviously been having, err ... *fun!*

Maybe you're even thinking about checking out the *original* versions of the Ten Best Ever horrors, or some other classic terror fiction. As the slime-spewing monster said to the screaming scientist... 'There's *plenty* more where *that* came from!'

But, before you do rush off to talk to your local fly-gobbling librarian or three-headed bookshop assistant, here's one final fact to make you gasp! *Some* people say that horror stories are just a cheap and easy way for writers to get a quick reaction from their readers. They also say that fear fiction is *totally* pointless and people would be better off spending their time reading something that is *good* for them! Well, as you've probably realized by now ... they're wrong! In addition to being fun, many fear fans find a regular dose of '*snap, cackle and chop*' a welcome relief from the *real* horrors of life. And as you may have already discovered, there are quite a few of them! Like the terrifying, Godzilla-sized, surprise spelling test that races into the classroom on a

Monday morning and seizes you by the brain cells ... *just* when you feel least able to handle it. Or the drooling, zombie-mutant PE teacher whose idea of a good time is to get everyone doing 50 laps of the playing field on a freezing January afternoon ... in a blizzard ... backwards ... in shorts.

So, what with the *real* world being full of so many *genuine* terrors, what could be better than relaxing with a few *pretend* nasties that you've got complete control over? It's all so *horribly* simple, isn't it? Scary story getting a bit *too* scary? Close the book! Movie monster got you shivering harder than a slug in a salt-shaker? Just flick the OFF switch! Cornered in your comfy chair by a rampaging Frankenstein monster with a neck the size of Norway? No problem! Just do what all the batty boffins do ... and make a bolt for it!